MW01706097

Peril on the Sea

THE TRINITY BAY DISASTER OF 1892

Peril on the Sea

THE TRINITY BAY DISASTER OF 1892

ELDON DRODGE

jesperson publishing

jesperson publishing

100 Water Street
P. O. Box 2188
St. John's, NL
A1C 6E6

National Library of Canada Cataloguing in Publication Data

Drodge, Eldon, 1942-
Peril on the Sea : The Trinity Bay disaster of 1892 / Eldon Drodge.

ISBN 1-894377-04-4

1. Trinity Bay (N.L.)--History--Fiction. 2. Sealing--Newfoundland and Labrador--Trinity Bay--History--Fiction. 3. Disasters--Newfoundland and Labrador--Trinity Bay--History--Fiction. I. Title.

PS8557.R62P47 2003 C813'.6 C2003-903705-3

Design/Layout: Freak Design

ALL RIGHTS RESERVED. No part of this work covered by the copyright hereon may be reproduced or used in any form or by any means—graphic, electronic or mechanical—without the prior written permission of the publisher. Any request for photocopying, recording, taping or storing in an information retrieval system of any part of this book shall be directed in writing to the Canadian Reprography Collective, 6 Adelaide Street East, Suite 900, Toronto, Ontario, M5C 1H6. This applies to classroom usage as well.

Printed in Canada.

To my mother, Cassandra Drodge,
who loved to tell stories
about Trinity Bay, and
Uncle "Lin" Ballett
who first told me about the
Trinity Bay disaster.

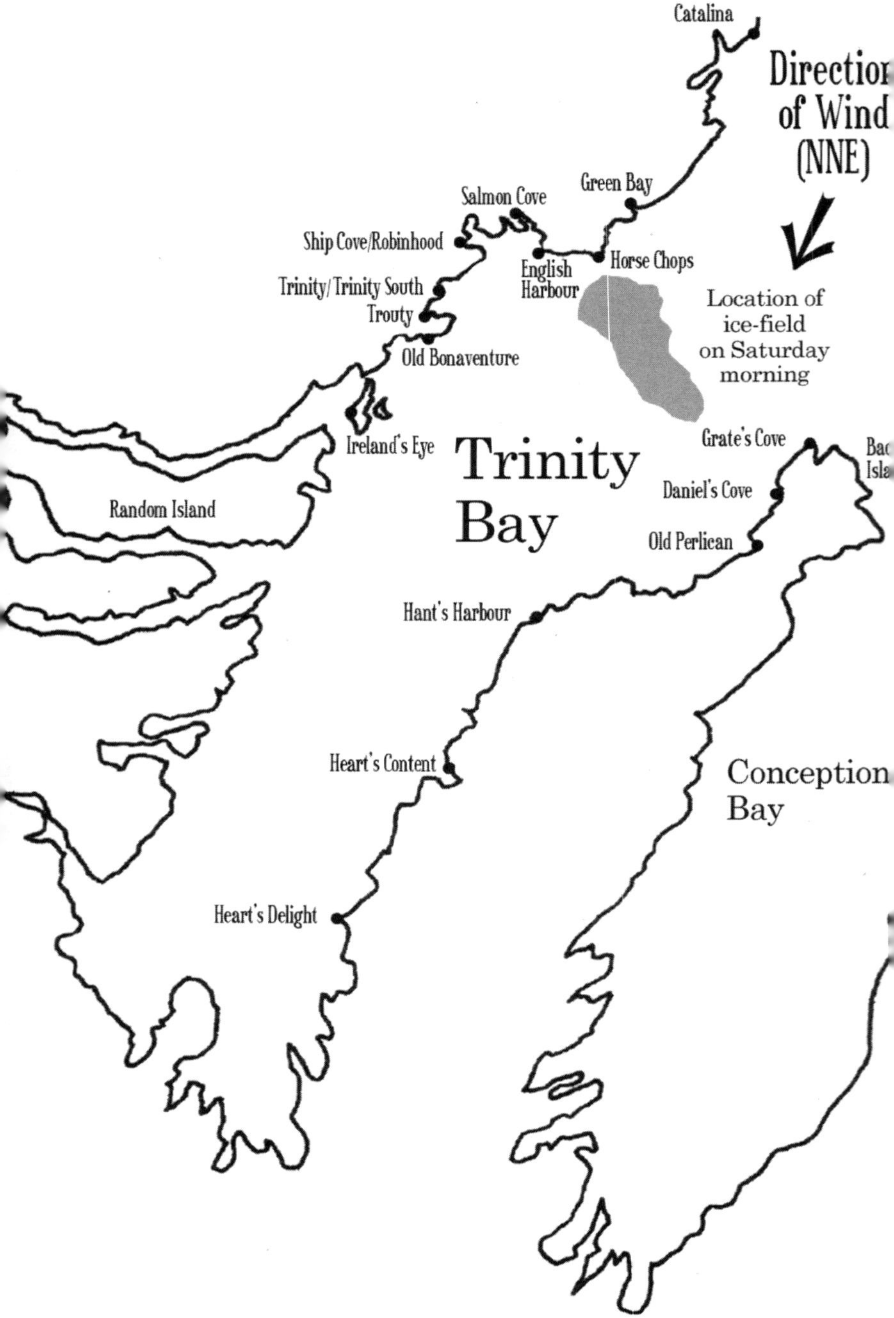
Catalina
Direction of Wind (NNE)
Green Bay
Salmon Cove
Ship Cove/Robinhood
English Harbour
Horse Chops
Trinity/Trinity South
Trouty
Location of ice-field on Saturday morning
Old Bonaventure
Ireland's Eye
Trinity Bay
Grate's Cove
Daniel's Cove
Old Perlican
Random Island
Hant's Harbour
Heart's Content
Conception Bay
Heart's Delight

Author's Note

This account of the Trinity Bay disaster of February 27th, 1892, is written in the form of a novel. While I have tried to remain true to the salient facts of the tragedy, my story is a dramatization of the events that occurred on that fateful day and should not be viewed as a document that is historically accurate in every respect. Some of the scenes of death and survival may not have occurred exactly as described. Specific information about the men who lost their lives in the disaster, the survivors, and other central characters, was gathered from newspaper accounts, other available documents, and word of mouth.

Eternal Father, strong to save,
Whose arm doth bind the restless wave,
Who bidd'st the mighty ocean deep
Its own appointed limits keep:
Oh, hear us when we cry to thee
For those in peril on the sea!

Eternal Father, Strong to Save
William Whiting 1825-78

CONTENTS

APPENDICES

I

The Swiles are In

Bob Bannister mopped up the last few morsels of boiled fish from his plate with a thick crust of bread, and washed the mixture down with a mouthful of hot tea. Pushing his chair back from the table, he went to the bottom of the stairs and called up to his son whom he suspected was still lying in bed trying to steal a few extra winks, "Charlie, come on b'y, the day is going to waste. If we don't get underway soon, it won't be worth our while going out at all. We might just as well stay home and do nothing."

The peevishness in his voice was plain, but he was just as vexed with himself as he was with Charlie. He had gotten out of bed at five o'clock that morning, well before daybreak, to check on the weather. He could tell even at that early hour that in all likelihood it was going to be a fine day. Hopefully, the ice would be in and conditions would be good enough for him to go out in the bay and try for a seal or two. With plenty of time to spare, the heavy quilts that he had just left looked so inviting that he had climbed back into the bed and nestled down beside his wife Flora again. He had meant to stay just a few minutes, but, despite his good intentions, had immediately drifted off to sleep again. To his great annoyance, he did not reawaken until after seven o'clock, much later than he had intended. He had hoped that he and Charlie would have been well out in the bay and perhaps nearing the ice-field by then, but now he knew that they would be well behind all the other men from the area who had undoubtedly gotten up and left at a much earlier hour.

"Yes, Da," came the muffled reply from upstairs, "I'm up. I'm just getting my clothes on. I'll be down in a few minutes. Tell mother to have a cup of tea ready for me."

Turning in exasperation to Flora, who had gotten out of bed with him to light the fire and to prepare his breakfast, Bannister grumbled, "That boy, I just don't know who he turns after. He's not like anyone else in this family, that's for sure. I expect he'll be late for his own funeral. I daresay everyone else in the bay is already out there by now. By the time we get out there, if we can ever get Charlie out of bed, there probably won't be a seal left to be had."

Flora Bannister knew her husband and his ways well. "Now Bob," she chided him gently as she always did whenever he was irritated or out of sorts, or appeared to be on the verge of one of his frequent outbursts, "Keep your patience. He's coming. You go on down to the stage and get the punt ready. By the time you're ready to leave, Charlie will be there. I'll see to it."

"Besides," she added, "you've got a good long day ahead of you, and a nice one too, by the look of it. And if what Skipper Fowlow said is right, there'll be more than enough seals for everybody no matter what time you get out there. It looks so calm and peaceful, I think I'd like to be going out in the bay with you myself just for the ride. So go on now, stop your grumbling and get your stuff together and get started."

A few minutes later Bannister, with a spritely stride that belied his sixty-two years, was making his way down the narrow road toward his fishing stage. There his small fifteen-foot punt lay waiting, hauled up on the beach near the sheltered side of the wharf. The warm sun felt good on his body, lifting his spirits and momentarily helping him to forget his annoyance with Charlie. Nestled in the crook of his arm was the aged muzzle loader that had been handed down to him by his father, and slung over his shoulder was his powder horn, inherited with the gun, containing what he hoped would be enough gun powder for the day ahead. He carried a coil of rope and two sealing gaffs as well. The latter would be needed to help himself and Charlie navigate their way over the shifting ice and around any open water areas that they might encounter, and if necessary, to fend off the attack of any overly aggressive mother seal that might take it upon herself to defend her newly whelped baby. The rope would be a necessity for hauling the seal carcases back to the punt in the event that they were lucky enough to kill any.

As was his custom whenever he left the house to venture out into the bay, he took a few minutes to scan the sky and the water for any signs of impending bad weather or troublesome water conditions. Today, from his viewpoint in Robinhood,[1] the sky was relatively cloudless and the moderate easterly wind that had been blowing for the past few days had abated, leaving the great expanse of water that constituted Trinity Bay as calm and as flat as a sheet of glass. He fancied that the houses of Daniel's Cove and Old Perlican, some twenty miles distant on the opposite south side of the bay, were much nearer and more defined than he had ever seen them before, as if they were magnified and brought closer by the still morning air. Even though it was still only February 27th, typically

---

[1] Robinhood and Ship Cove were two small adjacent fishing communities on the north shore of Trinity Bay which were amalgamated in 1910 to form the community of Port Rexton, named for one of the first families to live in the area.

the coldest month of the winter, and not yet eight o'clock in the morning, he was already enjoying the warmth of the sun on his face and body. For the first time in months, he carried his heavy coat over his shoulders instead of wearing it, and his woolen cuffs were left in his pocket. It offered to be a fine day for swiling – a great day to be alive.

Passing the house of Jim Randell, he took note of the fact that no smoke rose up from the Randells' chimney, an indication that no one was yet stirring inside. That didn't surprise him very much because Jim Randell was, in Bannister's opinion, a shiftless, lazy man who did far less than his best to provide for his wife and family. Bob Bannister, among others in the community, considered the man to be a hangashore; the last fisherman to go out on the water in the day, the first one back, the one who didn't even bother to go out at all if the weather conditions were anything less than ideal – and the first one to grumble when things didn't go his way. Someone in the community had once described him as "Hard to Start," a nickname that had followed him ever since. Bannister often wondered how Jim's family managed to survive. He suspected that it was largely because they were helped along by others in the community who, like himself and Flora, often dropped off small items of food and clothing to Randell's wife Myra, because they suspected that she and her children were hungry and cold most of the time. Randell himself seemed oblivious to the charity extended to his family by other people, or if he were aware of it, didn't seem to resent it. Perhaps he even expected it and relied on it himself. In any event, Bannister would have been more than a little surprised to see Jim going out to the ice that day even though the weather and the water conditions in the bay were perfect and his family could certainly use the food.

On the other hand, Bannister would have been puzzled indeed if the next house in the lane, that of John Butler, his life-long friend and companion, had not shown some sign of activity by this hour of the day. As he expected, it did, for gray smoke from Butler's chimney rose straight up in the still morning air, and there was John waving to him from the kitchen window where he had obviously been scanning the weather conditions out in the bay as he himself had done only minutes earlier. Bannister, however, felt almost certain that John would not put in an appearance out on the ice that morning either, but for an entirely different reason than Jim Randell's. Three days earlier, John Butler's thirty-three year old brother-in-law, Joseph Penney, who lived in English Harbour, had died after a long and difficult struggle with consumption. The funeral service was scheduled for two o'clock that afternoon in St. Silas's Church in that community.

On top of that, on the same day Penney had passed away, Butler had had the additional misfortune of slicing off the tops of three of the fingers on his left hand while making wood shavings with a razor-sharp axe. The injury was serious enough to force him to make the three-mile boat trip across the Bight to Trinity to have it treated by Dr. White. The good doctor had cleaned the gaping cuts with alcohol, sewed up the badly injured fingers, coated them with ointment, bandaged them, and cautioned Butler to make sure that he didn't get them dirty or wet until they had a chance to heal, else he might lose them. Bannister knew that only these extenuating circumstances would keep John at home and away from the ice. Otherwise he was sure that Butler would be among the first to be out there on a fine day like this.

For many people, including Bob Bannister and his family, the arrival of the ice in Trinity Bay, coming from the far north each spring, was always an anticipated and welcomed occurrence. The ice, pushed southward each year by brisk northerly winds and the strong tides of the Labrador Current, usually brought with it large numbers of seals that served to supplement the sparse fish-laden diet of the families of the area. A bit of seal meat was a well appreciated diversion from their usual bland fare. The presence of ice in the bay this early in the year, though welcomed, was nevertheless a bit unusual. Usually it didn't show up until sometime in March, or even as late as April. Some years it did not come at all, or if it did, remained too far off from the shore to be of any practical value to the men of the bay, who had only their tiny oar-powered punts and little jib sails as a means of making their way out to it.

The inshore seal fishery was very important to many families all over Trinity Bay. The large sea-going sealing vessels which operated out of St. John's and Trinity to pursue the annual seal hunt in the Gulf of St. Lawrence and in the vast expanse of ocean off Newfoundland's northeast coast known as the Front, could usually count a small number of Trinity baymen among their crews. The vast majority of the fishermen of the bay, however, had to be content with participating in the seal fishery as landsmen because berths on the sealing vessels were at a premium. Hard to obtain, once gotten they were guarded like gold. Unlike the hunts carried out in the Gulf and at the Front, where the focus was on seal oil and the luxurious pelts of newly whelped white-coats to supply the fashion industries of America and Europe, the emphasis of the inshore seal fishery was squarely on food. It was the nourishment that the herd remnants that drifted this far south could provide for men and their hungry families during this difficult period that drew the men out there. If a fisherman could get a few extra cents from the local merchant for his seal pelts and blubber, so much the better, but the prospect of acquiring badly needed food for the hungry mouths at home was what prompted him to venture out onto the treacherous ice in the first place.

At this time of the year, the dark protein-rich seal meat was an important, if not vital, component in the diet of families all around the bay. By late winter or early spring most households were a bit "short" as their provisions of flour, molasses, butter and other basic food necessities were dwindling and beginning to run out. The potatoes, turnips, carrots, and other vegetables that they had grown in their own small gardens, along with berries of various kinds gathered the previous fall from the surrounding barrens, were usually also running low by then. The bulk of these staples had either been consumed or in many cases lost to frost. No matter what precautions men and women took to protect their stores, once the temperature in their root cellars and frigid storerooms dipped below the freezing point and stayed there for any extended period of time, some portion of whatever was stored there would invariably be frost-damaged and rendered inedible. Thus, the months of February and March were often referred to in communities throughout outport Newfoundland as, "the hungry months," a time of belt-tightening, scrimping, and in many cases outright gut-wrenching hunger for many people. So for those fortunate enough to be able to obtain it, a supper of seal-flippers complete with gravy and dumplings and whatever vegetables could be mustered during this difficult period, was probably a feast that surpassed any other meal they might eat during the entire year. Some years, though, the northern ice did not put in its anticipated appearance at all, or if it did, arrived late or did not bring with it seals in any significant numbers. When this occurred it posed great hardship and deprivation for many families and often a life and death struggle to survive until spring and warmer weather arrived.

Come April, conditions usually improved. By then, sea trout flooded back into the brooks and streams, and the turrs and other sea-birds that returned from their winter retreat to populate the bay in great numbers were easy prey for the fishermen with their guns and small boats. Also, it was the time of year when it was getting safe for fishermen to put their punts back in the water again to begin the new fishing season.

The winter of 1892, which was now nearing its end, had been an unusual yet very difficult one for the residents of the area. The first significant snowfall had occurred in late November before most people in the bay were properly braced for it, and the temperature had fallen well below the freezing point, remaining there until Christmas. Then in late December, a short temporary warm spell and two days of heavy rain had taken away the snow, only to be immediately followed by yet another sustained period of intense frost which left the ground frozen hard and dry, a condition which persisted through all of January and most of February. While the lack of snow was preferred by some people, its absence had a detrimental effect on many households for two reasons.

Firstly, the majority of the houses in the area were raised from the ground. They had been constructed on wooden shores or rock piles to prevent them from rotting prematurely and to provide for a storage area underneath.

Very few of them had basement walls or insulation of any kind, and when the frigid westerly and northerly winds whistled up through the cracks in the floorboards, as it had during most of the winter, it pervaded every nook and cranny of the houses above. Even when the wind slackened, the deep frost still permeated the floor and made it extremely difficult for those living there to keep themselves warm and comfortable. Normally, heavy hard-packed snow with its natural insulating qualities, when piled against the lower sides of the houses, provided some extra warmth by eliminating the lower drafts that otherwise penetrated up through the floor. The kitchen was usually the only room in the house that was kept warm on any kind of sustained basis. For the most part, the other rooms, including the bedrooms, were usually left unheated, providing very little comfort throughout the winter.

Many houses, including Bob Bannister's, where bedrooms were located directly above the kitchen, had small openings cut in their kitchen ceilings to allow some of the heat to rise and pass through into the rooms above. On the coldest winter nights, many parents in the area were in the habit of placing heated bricks and water bottles under the covers of the beds in the other upstairs bedrooms to warm the quilts and blankets before sending their young sons and daughters up for the night. Strategies like these were employed all over the bay by families trying to sustain as much heat as they could for their comfort.

The other significant and serious effect of the absence of snow was the difficulty that it posed for men when they were gathering firewood from the surrounding forests. Although such a condition made it easier for them to make the trek into the woods and facilitated the actual cutting of the wood, hauling the cut logs out to their homes was quite another matter. Dog teams and horses were hard-pressed to drag even the smallest loads of firewood over the dry, rock-hard ground. Consequently, extremely small loads and countless trips were often necessary to achieve the same result that could have been easily accomplished in only a trip or two on snow covered ground, over which iron-shod sleds could pass with minimal effort.

Still, the warmth of the sun and the beauty of the morning had all but driven the severity of the current winter from Bob Bannister's mind. His thoughts were now focused on the present, and the prospect of obtaining a seal or two for the larder. Two days earlier Captain Richard Fowlow, returning to Ship Cove from Bonavista after delivering a cargo of lumber there, had reported that a large ice-field lay about ten or twelve miles offshore, stretching from Elliston to English Harbour. Having sailed his schooner, the ***Rosscleer***, close enough to it to get a good look, he was able to report that the ice was, "maggoty with swiles as far as I could see." This was welcome news which spread to every community around the bay within the space of a few hours. Most men knew, or hoped, that the slight easterly breeze which had been blowing for much of the previous few days should soon push the ice field close enough to land to enable the inshore fishermen in their small punts to easily reach it and its treasure-trove of seals.

As Bannister neared his fishing stage with these thoughts in mind, he glanced back over his shoulder and sure enough, there was Charlie, as Flora had promised, bounding along trying to catch up with him. He saw that

Charlie was carrying a grub sack that Flora had undoubtedly filled with the usual slabs of bread and a bottle of fresh water. Bannister hadn't thought about taking the grub bag himself. It wouldn't have mattered in any event for he, like most other men in the area, was accustomed to long hours of hard physical outdoor labour with very little food in his stomach. All he really needed to keep him going was a good breakfast in the morning and a hot supper waiting for him when he returned home in the evening. Anything else of an edible nature that came his way in between was a bonus.

Despite his constant grumbling, Bannister loved his son dearly. Charlie was the youngest of his eight children and both he and Flora, in their softer moments, had often been known to say that, "God sent us Charlie to be a comfort and a blessing to us in our old age." Charlie was clearly his father's favourite. From the time he could toddle around, Charlie had been his constant shadow, and Bannister, impatient as he was, had always taken the time to answer the boy's endless questions. He had always taken pains to explain things to him and to teach him the proper way to do certain jobs and tasks. He had also tried to instill in his son some of the virtue, decency and integrity that he himself possessed. Charlie, now eighteen, and his sister Isabelle were the Bannisters' only offspring still living at home. The others, daughters Mary Ann, Sarah, Selina, and Patience, along with sons John and Job, were all married and had left home to raise their own families.

Charlie had attended school until he was thirteen years of age, and was the only one in the family who could read and write with any degree of proficiency. His literary prowess manifested itself in many ways. At the age of ten, he had taken his father's powder horn and, with an awl, inscribed an intricate crisscross pattern of his own design on it, along with the words, "Property of Robert Bannister and sons, Robinhood, 1884." He had then painstakingly scrubbed ochre into the letters to make them stand out. From an early age he also kept a journal in which he recorded daily events, and he was constantly on the look out for new things to read. He was the one who wrote out the long letters that his mother regularly dictated to be mailed to her relatives in St. John's and other parts of Newfoundland, and he was the one who read the Bible and the little Trinity Bay newspaper, the *Weekly Record*, to his parents whenever they were able to obtain a copy. Bannister knew that Charlie was a good boy with a kind heart and was certainly a hard worker. He only wished that the boy would show a little more initiative and be a little more punctual about things.

II
The Exodus

John Butler, as Bob Bannister had correctly surmised, did not venture out to the ice-field with the others that day, although not from any lack of trying on his part. Despite his brother-in-law's funeral scheduled for that afternoon and the injury to his own hand, he had fully intended doing so. But when his wife, Mary, had awakened just before daylight and found her husband's place next to her in the bed empty, she had immediately guessed what was going on. She could hear him rummaging around downstairs in the kitchen, so she quickly got out of bed herself and went down to confront him. There he was, sitting at the table finishing off the last of his breakfast, and just as she suspected, he was wearing his sea-boots, a thick flannel shirt, and the heavy woolen guernsey that he always wore for outdoor work. She had caught him just in time.

"It's a good thing I came down when I did," she thought to herself, "another few minutes and he would have been through the door and heading out in the bay, and there wouldn't be a thing I could do about it."

"Where in the world do you think you're going?" she demanded.

John knew this wasn't going to be easy. "I'm going out in the bay like everybody else to see if I can get a swile or two," he responded, "that's where I'm going. Don't worry, I'll be back in plenty of time for the funeral."

It was the answer she had anticipated although she hadn't expected him to be so direct. Usually, when he was trying to put something over on her, he beat about the bush a lot more before coming to the point. She decided she would give him no leeway. "You foolish old bugger, John," she started, "you haven't got the sense God gave a louse. You know there's no bloody way you can row all the way out there by yourself and be back in time for the funeral. So have a grain of common-sense, b'y, and forget it. Go on back to bed."

Despite the fact that he knew in his own mind that the words of his sharp-tongued wife cut very close to the truth, he still tried to convince her otherwise. The chance of taking a seal or two was not a thing to be passed up lightly, funeral or no funeral. There probably wouldn't be any more good opportunities this winter and he didn't want to miss this one, no matter what. He'd look after his injured fingers as best he could.

"I can do it, Mary. There's not much of a sea running and the going will be easy. I won't stay very long and if I can't get a seal right off the bat, I'll just turn around and come back in again. I promise."

Mary changed tactics. "I know you never liked Joe, but the least I expected was that you'd have the decency to come to his funeral, after all he's your brother-in-law. My God, John, how can you be so callous? What will it look like with me and the youngsters there in church, but not you? What will people think? It's not like he was a total stranger, you know."

Mary often resorted to what she perceived to be John's dislike for his in-laws whenever she sensed that she was beginning to get on the losing end of any argument with him. Her strategy invariably worked because, as she intended, he was often made to feel guilty when she took this approach. In truth, he had never, as she intimated, really thought very much of most of Mary's relatives, especially her brother Joe. Another tactic that she sometimes employed was to threaten to take herself and the children up to her mother's house and remain there until John could see the light of whatever was the issue at the time and come to terms with her – and John understood her well enough to know that the stubborn and headstrong Mary was as likely as not to follow through and do exactly as she had threatened.

Interpreting John's lack of response as an indication that she was making progress, she pressed forward. "And what about your fingers? Don't you remember what Dr. White told you? You know full well that if you get them cuts full of old blubber and slub, you'll lose your full fingers – not just the tips. Or worse still, perhaps your hand. Then you'll end up being a cripple for the rest of your life. Is that what you want?"

She paused to let that much sink in, then added, "Besides, how would you ever manage to row all the way out there and back with a hand like that anyway? And all for the sake of a foolish old seal. We'll manage quite well without it, thank you. Alexander and Jimmy will look after us anyway, you know that as well as I do."

Alexander Butler was the youngest of John's four brothers and Jimmy was Alex's fifteen-year-old son. John was very fond of Jimmy – perhaps his favourite nephew – and often took him out fishing with him. Alex and his family lived just a few doors away in the same community, and again Butler knew in his heart that what Mary was saying would indeed be the case. Alexander, who was fully aware of John's predicament, would certainly give him and Mary a share of whatever he brought back from the ice that day.

His last feeble offer to get someone to come with him to do the rowing also fell on deaf ears. So, realizing that this was yet another argument that he couldn't possibly win no matter what he said, John conceded defeat and reluctantly abandoned his plans to go out to the ice. Still, he wouldn't grant her the satisfaction of victory. "Okay maid, have it your way. But don't blame me if we haven't got a bite to eat in the house later on. It won't be my doing when we're scravelling for something to put on the table."

For the next two hours he remained at the kitchen window watching as the little boats left the cove one by one, to begin the long row out to the ice. Even from this distance he could identify them all individually as well as most of the men and boys in them. He looked at his bandaged hand and cursed his bad luck. If his hand hadn't been injured as seriously as it was, he probably would have gone out with them regardless of what Mary might say about her brother Joe's funeral. Ironically, although he had no way of knowing it at that moment, later in his life he would sometimes look at the mangled tips of his fingers and think about the accident that had caused them in an entirely different light. Even though it had been excruciatingly painful at the time and had prevented him from going out seal hunting with the others, in retrospect he would come to realize that his misfortune had in all likelihood saved his life and enabled him to live to a relatively old age. He would eventually see it as a strange twist of fate, or an act of God, that had kept him on shore that day to save the lives of some of the men he now saw making their way out to the ice-field.

From his vantage point in the kitchen window, he saw that one of the first punts out on the water that morning was that of Nathaniel Penny, one of his wife's first cousins, another of the Pennys that he didn't like very much. He and Nathaniel had crossed paths before on a few occasions, and he now tried to avoid the man as much as possible. He recognized the man with Penny as Frederick Randell. He thought that was a bit odd because he had never known those two men to have ever buddied up before. He wondered what caused them to throw in their lot together this time.

Not far behind Penny and Randell came the Stockley brothers, William and Arthur, and a few minutes behind them Alexander and Jimmy in their small fifteen-foot punt. They in turn were followed by a steady stream of others during the next hour or so, until John Butler was convinced that he was the only man left on shore – with the exception of "Hard to Start" Randell, who was undoubtedly still at home curled up in his bed. Then he remembered that he hadn't noticed Bob Bannister's boat among the others. He had seen Bob heading down toward his fishing stage earlier, but now he wondered if Bob had taken sick or something because he couldn't fathom his friend missing a good opportunity like this unless something was wrong. The thought had scarcely crossed his mind when he saw Bannister's punt, with Bob and his son in it, heave into view. "Must have been Charlie holding things up again," he muttered to himself, "as usual."

Farther out in the bay, much too far away to be able to identify them individually, he saw many other small boats on their way to the ice-field. He speculated that they were men from the communities of Trinity, Trinity East, Goose Cove, Cuckhold's Cove,[2] and Trinity South,[3] and perhaps

---

[2] Renamed Dunfield in 1910.
[3] The South Shore of Trinity.

from as far away as Trouty and the Old and New Bonaventures. Turning away in disgust at his own situation, he put on his coat and left the house to walk somewhere, anywhere, just to get out of the house for a few minutes.

In Salmon Cove[4] and English Harbour, two other small fishing settlements situated a little farther to the north, a similar exodus was taking place as men from these communities also made their way out to the ice-field in their tiny boats. These men did not have quite as far to row as their counterparts from Robinhood, Ship Cove, and the other settlements that lay immediately to their south because the ice-field at that moment lay only three and a half miles off the Horse Chops, the headland of a stretch of rugged coastline that extended from English Head northward for about ten miles to the settlement of Catalina. The ice was much closer to the Horse Chops than anywhere else in the bay.

Among the little flotilla of punts converging on the ice was that of twenty-eight year-old Bill Day, who had left his house in Salmon Cove at quarter to seven, one of the first men out on the water that morning. Accompanying him was his younger cousin, Charles Day, who had just turned twenty. These two men had fished and worked together for the past two years and despite a great difference in their personalities and sizes, got along well with each other. They enjoyed each other's company for the most part, and made an effective two-man fishing crew. Even though there was usually only the two of them, they utilized a twenty-one foot punt of the bigger

---

[4] Renamed Champneys in 1904 to eliminate confusion with several other Salmon Coves in other areas of Newfoundland.

"four-handed" variety normally employed by larger crews.

Bill Day, at six-foot-four, was one of the biggest men in Trinity Bight, with a mouth, some said, to match his huge frame. Loud and argumentative, he usually got what he wanted through bullying, intimidation, and aggression, and had been known to use his fists on more than a few occasions to make sure he got his own way. Paradoxically, he was generally seen to be a good family man and a good provider for his wife and children. Despite his crude manner and overly aggressive nature, many people in the area gave him credit for that if nothing else. Still, most gave him a wide berth when they saw him coming. Only his diminutive wife, Sarah, could keep him under control. Nobody knew how she managed it but she had him under her thumb and was somehow able to rule him with an iron hand. Whatever she told him to do he did meekly and without question. It was a well known fact in the Bight that he had never once raised his hand or his voice against his wife in their seven years of marriage, or against any of their three small children.

In keeping with his great bulk, he was a work-horse, an extremely strong man who could toil away at the hardest physical labour from the first light of day until nightfall in all kinds of weather, pausing only occasionally to take a short rest. His feats of strength and endurance were well known all around the bay. He was a handy man to have around when boats had to be pulled up on the beach or heavy objects had to be lifted or moved. Through his hard labours and perseverance, he had built and maintained for himself and his family one of the finest and sturdiest houses in Salmon Cove, set well back on the highest point of land in the community to give him an unobstructed view of the bay. For Bill Day, this hard, belligerent, strong, complex man, the effort of rowing out to the ice-field and harvesting a few seals would be mere child's play.

By contrast, his partner and cousin, Charles Day, was much shorter and very slight of build. He was also shy, retiring, and passive almost to the point of being a recluse. The two men were such an unlikely pair that it was difficult to understand how they worked so well together and were as successful in their endeavors as any other two-man fishing crew in the bay. Surprisingly, Charles didn't seem to mind his partner's overly assertive behaviour and didn't let it bother him very often. He had long since gotten used to Bill's frequent taunts and threats to scuttle him or to throw him overboard, and no longer paid them any heed. His biggest fear now when they were out on the water together was Bill's habit of perching his great body on the gunnel of the punt whenever he wanted to have a smoke, an action that invariably sent the small boat heeling over sharply on that side almost to the point of capsizing. Charles always feared that it would be the very moment when some larger than usual wave would catch them broadside and swamp them. The first time it happened, Charles had cautioned Bill to be more careful. Bill's only response had been to violently rock the boat from side to side until Charles was sure they were going under, so he never mentioned it again. Now Bill, oblivious to the danger that his actions presented, continued to smoke his pipe there day after day in perfect peace and contentment.

A few weeks earlier Charles had confided to Bill that he was going to marry Emma Bailey from Cuckhold's Cove in June. It was a confidence that he soon regretted sharing with the other man because ever since then Bill had, whenever the two of them were alone, tried to pry out of him the most intimate details of his relationship with Miss Bailey. Bill teased him mercilessly about his upcoming marriage and tried to enlighten him in the most graphic and explicit manner on how to fulfil his responsibilities in the marriage bed once he was wed. Seldom a day would pass without Bill asking him something like, "How did you ever work up the nerve to ask her in the first place, Charl? You sly devil," or, "I never thought you had it in you, b'y," and would then guffaw loudly at his own crude attempt at humour.

Whenever Bill carried on like that, Charles tried to focus his full attention on whatever task was at hand to blot out the other man's jeers and provocations, and to let him know that he wasn't interested in responding to anything that he was saying. Still, although he was sometimes a bit embarrassed and uncomfortable with some of Bill's jibes, he really didn't mind them all that much when the two of them were alone. It was only when they were delivered in the presence of other people that they really bothered him. Then he usually had to bite his tongue to refrain from retaliating. Still, his relationship with Bill Day was one of the few real ones that he had ever been able to cultivate in his lifetime, and he didn't want to do or say anything to jeopardize it. Now, as they neared the ice-field, his thoughts were squarely on the prospect of what might lie ahead.

III
On the Ice

By nine-fifteen, after an hour and a quarter of non-stop rowing, Bob and Charlie Bannister were within a quarter-mile of the ice-field. Earlier they had both taken off their heavy jackets, woolen cuffs, and leather caps and placed them in the stern of the punt for safekeeping. Having been subjected to the bitter cold of the winter for so long, they intended to make the most of the unseasonably fine weather while it lasted. The temperature in the last half hour or so had, however, dropped noticeably and the earlier glassy condition of the water of the bay was now broken by small waves and a rising swell created by the gentle easterly breeze that had sprung up. Even though the weather was not quite as pleasant as it had been earlier in the morning, it was still a reasonably fine day by normal standards for this time of the year, and neither Bob nor Charlie yet felt cold or uncomfortable enough to retrieve their warmer clothing and put it on again. Father and son, content to be out on the water under such good weather conditions, rowed together in perfect unison without any wasted motion or conscious effort. Because they were such expert oarsmen, their skill honed to perfection through long hours of practice, their punt glided efficiently through the water at a steady, sustained pace as it approached its destination.

On the way out, their sporadic conversation had centered on the usual things – jobs and chores that had to be done around the house and things of interest that were happening within the rest of the family, as well as topical matters of note around the Bight. Mostly, though, they discussed ways in which Charlie should try to improve himself and his circumstances. For some reason, Bob had of late gotten it in his head that it was about time his youngest son started to consider his future. After all, the boy would be twenty in a couple of years, a time when any young man should be starting to think about getting married and beginning a family of his own. And Charlie, who to his father's knowledge had not yet even courted a girl, had done very little to give his father any expectations in this regard. So far, he had resisted the advances of several girls in the Bight who clearly had their sails set for him, for he was a good looking young man and a fine physical specimen and by all accounts was as good a catch as there was in the area. One young girl in particular, sixteen-year-old Clara Ballett, appeared to be more determined than the others and frequented the Bannister home on a regular basis. She was never deterred or put off by Charlie's obvious lack of interest in her, perhaps hoping that time and familiarity would eventually win him over. Even if Charlie wasn't interested, she had made an impression on at least one person in the house, for Flora Bannister, although she never spoke openly about it, often thought Clara might someday make a good wife for her youngest son.

"He's got it too good at home, that's the trouble," thought Bob Bannister to himself. "He'll never leave the nest as long as me and Flora are treating him as good as we are. We've got to make him do more things for himself. That's the only way to make him show some initiative."

When they had exhausted their conversation about Charlie's shortcomings and love life, or lack of one, they discussed the new addition that they planned to make to their small fishing stage in the spring. "We got to get 'er done this year, Charlie b'y, so we'll have a bit more room. We can't leave it much longer. We're so cramped for space now we can hardly turn around in there, let alone store a paying voyage of fish. And those two end shores will need replacing soon. They're eaten out pretty badly."

While rowing, Bob had also made a mental note to himself that when the weather got a little warmer he would have to make a few repairs to the punt to try to make her last another year or two. He and Charlie had always been very open and at ease with each other, and unlike many other father and son combinations who worked together for days on end in relative silence, their own workday was usually filled with intermittent chatter and conversation. If at other times they felt no compulsion to talk, the two of them just worked quietly side by side, lost in their own individual thoughts.

As they made their final approach to the ice-field, Charlie remarked, "That looks like the Batsons'[5] punt pulled up on the ice over there, Da. And I think that's Bob Fowlow's just beyond it. I wonder if Edgar is out with him." Edgar was Fowlow's seventeen-year-old son and one of Charlie's closest friends. Taking note of the reddened ice in the area of the Fowlows' punt, he added, "looks like they've got a seal or two already. They've probably been out here a while, I daresay."

Unable to resist the temptation to get in yet another gentle barb at his lackadaisical son, Bannister answered, "I'd say you might be right about that, Charlie b'y. You can rest assured that they weren't at home curled up in bed

---

[5] The different spellings of Batson, Betson, and Bestone appear to have been used interchangeably during that time period.

at all hours like some people I know, not mentioning any names of course. But like they say, the early bird gets the worm."

The Batsons that Charlie had referred to were William and Arthur Batson from English Harbour. They were brothers who had both married women from the immediate area, built their homes and raised their families next door to each other in English Harbour, and had worked and fished together ever since. Both men were deeply religious. Arthur, aged thirty-eight, was especially devout and usually took it upon himself to conduct church services whenever the minister of the parish, who usually came to English Harbour to preach one Sunday of every month, was not in attendance. And now he and William, like almost every other able-bodied man in the community, were out to take full advantage of the God-sent opportunity to go out and get a seal or two to feed their families.

This morning, for one of the very few times in their married lives, Arthur and his wife, Elizabeth, had not kissed each other or said goodbye before he left home to go out in the bay. When he was ready to leave, she was still sleeping, which was a rarity since she was usually the first one out of bed every morning. And he, reluctant to wake her, had left as quietly as possible to avoid disturbing her or the children. With their youngsters and all the work that had to be done, it wasn't very often that she had an opportunity to get a little extra sleep. It was a few extra minutes of sleep, however, that Elizabeth Batson would regret for the rest of her life.

As he headed out to the ice in the punt with his brother, Arthur took advantage of the time to focus his thoughts on what he might try to include in his sermon for tomorrow morning's church service. It would be another two weeks before the Reverend John Godden, the Church of England Minister for the parish, would be in English Harbour to conduct the service, and Arthur, as usual, would be expected to take over in his absence. Among Arthur's favourite and most frequently used sermons were those of Jesus walking on the Sea of Galilee and Paul being shipwrecked on his way to deliver his message of Christianity to the Romans. He always liked to have a theme of the sea running through his sermons.

William Batson, Arthur's older brother by a year, was lost in his own thoughts and rowed in silence beside him. Before he left home that morning, William's wife of fifteen years, Taffita, whom he revered above all others, had, unlike Elizabeth Batson, risen with him to get him his breakfast and to tell him, as she always did whenever he left to go out on the water, that she loved him and urged him to be careful while he was out there. He always looked back upon his marriage to Taffita as the best thing that had ever happened to him. Wild, restless, and independent in his younger years, he had gradually been influenced by the love and caring of his young wife until now she and their children were the center of his existence. Little else mattered.

By nine-thirty that morning, Saturday, February 27th, 1892, on what would later turn out to be one of the most fateful days in the history of Trinity Bay, the bay was alive with activity. No fewer than two hundred men and boys and upwards of eighty small boats had rowed out from communities as far north as Green Bay and as far south as Ireland's Eye, every man with the same objective in mind – to kill a few seals and bring them home to feed himself and his hungry family.

They came in small punts – one, two, three or four men

to a boat, sometimes more. The sturdy little round-bottomed, narrow-keeled boats that bore them varied greatly in size. Some were extremely small, in some cases no more than twelve or thirteen feet in length, while some of the larger boats exceeded twenty feet or more. These landsmen, now seal hunters for this occasion, used the same boats to make their livelihoods in the cod-fishery during the warmer months. They were the backbone of the fishing-based economy of Newfoundland, yet they seldom had a cent in their own pockets. At the same time, the fishing merchants to whom they supplied their catches grew enormously wealthy and powerful on the fruits of their labours.

Some of these little boats, squat and ugly, reflected the limited ship-building skills of their owners. Most, however, were reasonably well shaped and quite passable in terms of their lines and symmetry, while still others, the best among them, could be considered true works of art and beauty. These had been built by a handful of talented men scattered around the bay who were deemed to be the very best in the area at their craft. Some of these gifted craftsmen, like sixty-year-old Harvey Toope of Cuckhold's Cove, rarely had to venture out onto the salt water themselves as they were able to make a good living by building boats for others. Money rarely exchanged hands in these transactions, but these craftsmen were able to get by just as well on what they received in kind for their boats, as they would have if they had been fishermen out on the water themselves. The fish, wood, animals, wool, oil, vegetables, hours of labour, and other items bartered by the fishermen, filled their every need. It was a matter of pride to fishermen all over the bay to be able to boast that they were the owners of a Toope-built punt. Toope and the few other master boatbuilders in the area always had a long backlog of requests for their boats, and it wasn't just a matter of placing an order with them. Everybody had to wait their turn. Because of the heavy demand, orders sometimes took upwards of two or three years to be filled and the men seeking them had to be patient. Toope and the other boat-builders, with their reputations for craftsmanship on the line, would not be rushed. Everyone knew his place on the waiting list, and if there was the slightest hint of anyone trying to jump the queue, a racket would invariably ensue to get the matter straightened out as quickly and as fairly as possible.

Built of spruce from the nearby forests, caulked with oakum to keep them tight and seaworthy, and smeared over with pitch and tar to prevent them from rotting out in the water, these tiny punts were the workhorses of the inshore fishing industry at the time. The smaller ones were typically two-oared, or "two-handed," boats in which the owner sat on the single tawt amidship to row while the rest of the space in the small craft, with the exception of smaller tawts in the stern and the bow, was reserved for holding fish and storing the necessary fishing gear. Sometimes two men sat side by side to do the rowing (and perhaps the talking), or one of them might use a third oar, a longer sculling oar, in the stern to assist the punt in its progress and to steer it. Most of these little boats also carried a small jib sail to take advantage of any trailing wind to let themselves be pushed along, thus permitting the men onboard to take a spell or relax for a while.

The larger punts were mostly four-oared boats with two tawts amidship to accommodate up to four rowers, depending on how many men were in the punt at the time. Typically, three or four-man fishing crews worked these slightly bigger boats throughout the fishing season.

Every fall, most of the boats were pulled out of the water, turned upside down, and stored for the winter. But on that Saturday morning, February 27th, many of them were quickly made ready for action by their owners, because by then every man in the bay could see that overnight the large field of ice had drifted much farther south and much closer to the land. By first light Saturday morning its northernmost edge was positioned directly off the Horse Chops while its southernmost edge stretched three-quarters of the way across the mouth of Trinity Bay to the vicinity of Old Perlican on the south shore. The ice-field, almost twenty miles wide, also extended eastward out into the open Atlantic Ocean for a further distance of some seven or eight miles, making it an immense body of ice by any stretch of the imagination. Hopefully, it had brought with it seals in sufficient numbers to satisfy the expectations of the hungry landsmen who had come out en masse in their small punts to hunt them.

By nine-thirty, the ice-field was littered with punts from end to end, and crawling with men and boys armed with gaffs, clubs, axes, muzzle loaders, and other weapons of all shapes and sizes. As the sealers had hoped, adult harp seals and their off-spring white coats abounded, interspersed with an occasional hood seal, the largest and most ferocious of the species. The men from Salmon Cove and English Harbour, who because of their closer proximity to the ice-field had been able to row out to their destination in less than an hour, had been the first to reach the ice-field. Those who came from communities farther away, like Old Bonaventure, New Bonaventure, and Ireland's Eye, had taken upwards of two hours or more in some cases to reach the more southern areas of the ice-pack.

The hunt for seals was in full swing. Blood painted the ice red where they had been killed and butchered as soon as they were sighted. Other catches were hauled back to the punts untouched and the butchering left to be done later. Small piles of dead seals lay everywhere as men tried to take full advantage of the harvest while the good weather lasted. Many seal hunters did not have to travel very far from the spot where they had landed their punts to find success, while others who had landed at less advantageous points sometimes had to travel much farther out over the ice-field, sometimes as much as two or three miles, in search of their quarry.

Despite their plentiful numbers, the seals were not an easy catch. Most of them fled immediately by slipping down into the nearest open water area whenever they were approached. Even the newly-whelped white-coats could sometimes sense the presence of danger and flee as well. Those that didn't were usually defended by their mothers, fierce creatures that when aroused would go to any lengths to protect their young. On the treacherous, ever shifting ice with its rafters and pitfalls of soft spots and open water areas, a man had to be quick and nimble indeed to be a successful seal hunter. More than a few of them had unexpectedly found themselves up to their necks in the frigid salt water in their attempts. Still, for the majority of the men who were out there at the time, the morning thus far had been successful, and most of them could boast at least a seal or two for their efforts.

IV
Storm Coming On

Among the last to arrive at the ice-field that morning were Eliol Tavener and his eleven-year-old grandson Eric. They had left their home in Trinity South at about the same time as most of the other men and boys from their community but, unlike the others, Tavener had chosen to take his time at the oars. Being seventy-one years of age, Tavener wanted to conserve his strength and energy for the seal hunt ahead and the long row back. Eric, with strict orders from his mother to, "stay close to Pop and don't do anything foolish or you'll hear it from me when you get home," sat impatiently in the stern of the punt.

"Come on, Pop," he urged, "try to go a bit faster. The other boats are pulling away from us, and they're going to get all the seals. There'll be nothing left for us."

"Now, Eric, be patient," the old man replied, "we'll be there in plenty of time. There's no need to rush."

"What about if I do the rowing?" the boy persisted, "I know I can row a lot faster than you."

The old man laughed softly. "If I turned these oars over to you, my son, we might never get there at all. Or, better yet, we might end up in Smith's Sound or somewhere like that, the way you row. Now just sit there and mind your gob or I'll turn around and take you home and come back out by myself."

Eric had been out in the bay fishing many times before with his grandfather and uncles while his father was working in St. John's as a carpenter. But this was the first time he had ever been permitted to accompany anyone out to the ice-packs looking for seals. He was excited and anxious to get there and determined to make his first kill. Despite the boy's prodding, Tavener, a wizened old veteran of the sea, was in no rush and not about to let himself be cajoled or bullied into trying to do anything beyond his intent and capability. There would be seals enough for all, he was certain, and if there weren't, so be it. It wouldn't be the end of the world. In any event his slight frame and aging body could do no better.

Eric, now resigned to the fact that he wouldn't be able to get his grandfather to go any faster, turned his questions to the business of killing seals. "How do you do it, Pop? How come you never brought your gun with you like the other men?"

"We don't need a gun, Eric," Tavener answered, "they're nothing but trouble. We're better off without it." In the old man's experience, a sealing gaff was all that was needed for killing white-coats. Killing adult seals, though, was quite another matter. For that, a gun was required, because a three or four hundred pound harp seal, when wounded or cornered, could inflict serious damage. On the other hand, all it took to send a white-coat to a quick and merciful death was one well-aimed blow with the gaff to the soft spot on its head.

Having been among the last to get out to the ice-field, Eliol and Eric would also be among the first to leave that morning and head back home. Almost immediately upon arrival at the ice, they spotted a seal pup not more than fifty feet from the spot where they had landed. Checking first to make sure that its mother wasn't nearby, Tavener quickly killed the white-coat with his gaff and dragged it back to the punt. As he did so he felt the ice rise and fall alarmingly beneath his feet, and he knew immediately that an extremely heavy tide had begun to run.

Having spent most of his seventy-one years on the salt water, Tavener was long accustomed to the signs that usually preceded any sudden and serious deterioration in the weather. He instinctively realized that the sharp drop in the temperature and the black clouds that he saw hurtling toward them from the northeast meant that the best of the weather was over for that day. The shifting of the easterly wind to a more northerly direction, together with the sudden increase in the strength of the tides, were other telltale signs of rough weather rapidly approaching. His intuition told him that the best thing to do was head for home. If he had come out alone or with another grown man he might have decided to stay a while longer and take his chances, but with his grandson in his charge, coupled with his anxiety about the changing weather, he felt compelled to go back.

"Come on, Eric. Help me get the punt back into the water. We're going home. I don't like the look of this sky."

"But Pop," the young boy protested, "we've only just landed here and all we've got so far is that one little pup. That's not enough. I allow there's thousands more out here just waiting for us. We can't go back yet."

"Never mind that, my son. This little seal will do us for now. But if the ice stays in the bay for a few more days we'll come out again and try for a few more, I promise you. Now come here and help me get this punt off the ice."

Eric wasn't so easily deterred. "You go on back then if you want to, Pop. I can stay out and come back home later with Uncle Sol. That's him over there," he pleaded, pointing out three men a short distance away, one of whom was his uncle, Solomon Tavener.

"No, my son," the old man countered, "not a chance.

You came out with me and you're coming back with me. If I left you out here and anything happened to you, your mother would have my hide, let alone what your father would do to me when he got home. I'd never hear the end of it."

Eric still wasn't mollified, but after a few more feeble entreaties he reluctantly obeyed his grandfather and helped him move the punt into the water. Before leaving, Tavener called out to Solomon and some of the other men within hearing distance to express his concern about the changing weather conditions. "Better keep a good eye on the weather, b'ys," he cautioned them, "I think we got a big blow coming on."

The only response he got was a wave of Solomon's hand and a shout that he couldn't make out over the wind. A few minutes later the old man and the disgruntled boy were heading back toward Trinity South in water that was already becoming increasingly choppy and foam-ridden. The single white-coat that they had killed lay in the stern of the punt where they had slung it. It was not very much to show for the effort of rowing all the way out to the ice-field and back. Aware of Eric's keen disappointment, he told him, "It's better to be safe than sorry, my son." They were prophetic words that he would often recall in the weeks and months to come. Even Eric would later admit that, "I'm some glad Pop took me home when he did. God only knows where I'd be by now."

Eliol Tavener was a wise and cautious man by nature, but the fullness of the wisdom of his decision to abandon his search for seals and head back home so early that morning would not fully manifest until later that day. Although he had the sharpness to notice and take heed of the first signs of bad weather and the sense to obey his instincts, he had no real way of knowing that within the hour the area that he was now leaving would become a raging tempest – and the scene of one of the worse disasters ever known in the history of Trinity Bay.

For unbeknownst to Tavener and the other two hundred men who were out on the ice at that moment, not more than thirty miles to the north an intense low pressure weather system was bearing down on Trinity Bay with enormous force and breakneck speed. Having originated in the frigid northern latitudes of Baffin Bay a week earlier, the system had remained stalled a hundred miles north of the Bonavista Peninsula for several days until a second and even more powerful low pressure system spawned in the same area had caught up with it, reactivated it, and nudged it into motion again, sending it speeding southward in all its fury. By ten o'clock that morning it had passed over the cluster of Bonavista Bay settlements that lay directly to the north of the Trinity Bight area, and would in the space of the next hour or so advance into Trinity Bay itself.

Grizzled old Bonavista baymen in their eighties and nineties, who thought that they had seen everything that the elements had to offer in their time, would later say that they had never witnessed anything like it. One minute it had been almost as warm and calm as a summer's day, they claimed, and the next minute all hell had broken loose as the storm seemingly sprang out of nowhere and unleashed its sudden wrath on the area, catching the unsuspecting livyers by surprise and driving them into the shelter of their homes. Those who happened to be out on the water at the time had barely been able to make it back to the land in time. Eliol Tavener himself would say afterward that, "I knew there was a bit of weather coming on, but I never in my wildest dreams expected anything like that." His words probably spoke for every man in the bay.

A few of the two hundred men on the ice in Trinity Bay at the time had, like Eliol Tavener, spotted the early warning signs, heeded them, and headed for home. The vast majority of them, however, were so engrossed in their quest for seals that they had either failed to take notice of the indicators that existed, or if they had seen them at all, had simply ignored them until the storm was upon them. By then it was almost too late, for it was already rapidly deteriorating into a full scale winter gale that sent the temperature plummeting well below the freezing point, sent blinding snow squalls across the ice-field, and whipped the previously peaceful waters of the bay into a white-capped frenzy.

This sudden and catastrophic change in the weather had taken place in the space of no more than fifteen or twenty minutes, catching the vast majority of the men who were out on the ice at the time completely off-guard and leaving them no alternative but to try to make their way back to land as quickly and as best they could. Most of them immediately realized the seriousness of their situation and made straight for their punts. Some abandoned their seal catches where they were while others, determined to the end, tried to salvage what they could and attempted to drag their catches back with them. This foolhardy decision, for many, would cost them precious minutes that to their peril would soon afterward come back to haunt them.

Deceived by the unseasonably fine weather and the warm temperature of the early morning, many of the men were clad only in the slight clothing that they had donned on leaving home. Some who had the foresight to wear their heavier clothes, had discarded them in the heat of the hunt as the morning wore on and placed them somewhere close by on the ice to be retrieved later. On the now violently buckling ice and in the blinding snow, it was virtually impossible in many cases to locate many of these pieces of clothing again. Most items had either been blown away by wind squalls or had disappeared into the open water areas that suddenly materialized everywhere as the shifting ice-field began to break up. Now their owners had no choice but to try to make their way to shore clad only as they were at that moment. Only the fortunate few who had kept their warm clothing on during the hunt were in any way appropriately dressed for the mad dash for home.

Far less fortunate were those who had ventured out onto the outermost reaches of the ice-field in search of seals and were trapped long distances from their punts when the storm struck. They now had to try to backtrack over the treacherous ice as fast as they could – which was no easy feat in the brutal and rapidly deteriorating weather and ice conditions. Many became disoriented in the blizzard and had great difficulty finding their way back. As well, many seal hunters had not had the foresight to pull their punts well up onto the ice when they had arrived there in the first place. Now, when they finally located the area where they had left their boats they found to their dismay that they had been set adrift and were being blown away by the fierce wind which was by then howling from the north-east at gale force, and were thus left with no alternative but to try to seek passage with others.

Many of the punts that pulled away from the treacherous ice-field to escape the storm, especially the last ones to leave, were grossly overloaded. Sometimes as many as seven or eight men crammed into a single small "two-handed" boat, making it extremely vulnerable to capsizing or swamping in the heavy sea. Still, not a single man among them, despite the great danger to his own person, refused anyone else who was stranded and in dire need of passage to shore and safety.

By twelve noon the large ice-field, unable to withstand the enormous pressure of the tides underneath it, had become a place of extreme danger. Buckling and shifting and rafting in great layers in response to the colossal forces pressing upon it, it was very quickly rendered almost impassable for the men and boys still trapped on it. The ice parted everywhere, opening up sudden ponds of water that threatened to swallow the fleeing seal hunters or, at best, force them to cautiously navigate their way around the open water areas. The ice that only an hour or so earlier had been such a bountiful source of food for the landsmen and their families back home had in the space of an astonishingly short time become a deathtrap, a graveyard that would claim the lives of many of them before the day was done.

V
The First Casualties

William and Arthur Batson of English Harbour were stranded two and a half miles out on the ice-field when the storm struck. Although they had seen a small number of seals as they trudged out over the ice-pack, they hadn't bothered to stop to kill them. They had both been determined to search out what they jokingly referred to as the "main patch," a term normally applied in the offshore seal fishery to the largest concentration of seals on the vast northern ice-fields of Newfoundland and Labrador. When they found it, they planned to take as many seals as they could. Their search thus far had been relatively fruitless for they still hadn't found that heavier concentration that they were seeking. In the fashion of berry pickers not satisfied with the pickings around them and unable to resist the urge to move ever onward in search of bigger and better prospects, they had wandered farther and farther out onto the ice as the day progressed. Yet they still had nothing but sweating bodies and wet feet to show for their efforts.

William had convinced Arthur that when they found the main herd, as he knew they most assuredly would if they searched long enough, they would kill as many seals as possible. They would then secure their carcasses in a marked location and come back out the following day bringing their bobsled with them in the punt to haul the seals back to the edge of the ice. They had gambled that the ice-field would remain where it was for a while longer, and that the favourable weather would hold for at least another day. It was a calculated risk that they had both been willing to take in anticipation of far greater rewards if they were lucky enough to guess right. "Why settle for one or two," William had said, "when you can have the lot?"

Now the two men quickly came to the realization that they had probably gone a bit too far and might be in some trouble. They were a perilously long distance from where they had left their punt. Heavy driving snow was already obscuring their vision and preventing them from seeing much more than a few yards ahead. The sudden drop in the temperature was in sharp contrast to the warmer weather that had existed only a short time earlier, and the wind was beginning to blast their bodies with great force. To make matters worse, the ice beneath their feet was starting to buckle and shift violently with the pressure of the heavy tides running underneath it.

William was the first to broach the subject of abandoning their search for seals and making their way back to the punt. "It's starting to look pretty bad, Art, b'y. I daresay we should knock off and head back before it gets too much worse."

Arthur, as he usually did whenever difficult situations arose or hard decisions had to be made, deferred to the more assertive and self-confident William. His sudden nervousness and apprehension belied his calm outward appearance. "Tis going to be a pretty hard slog back to the punt in this blizzard, isn't it? Do you think we'll have any trouble finding our way? I don't think I'd like to have to spend the night out here."

The other man didn't commit himself. "I don't know, b'y," he offered, "but I think we'd better get started right away." His reply did not exactly ooze with the confidence that Arthur tried to detect in his voice in order to allay his own growing concern. “I think we’ll be alright,” William continued, “but it’s not going to be easy. Follow me and stay as close as possible. We don’t want to get separated from each other way out here.”

Both he and Arthur, like many of the other landsmen who had elected to leave their heavier winter garments at home that morning, were already wet and chilled to the bone. William knew that the wind had swung around northerly but he did not know to what extent. Their visibility was already extremely limited, but he reasoned that if they just kept walking into the teeth of the wind they ought to be generally heading in the right direction. They might have to narrow down their search for their punt when they reached the innermost edge of the ice-pack, but now their first priority was to make it that far. Hopefully, when they got there they would be able to see the land and get their bearings.

They set off together, their shoulders hunched into the wind and their heads bent to lessen the impact of the wind and the driving snow on their faces. They both knew that it was going to tax every bit of their strength and endurance to make it back to their punt. Even when they got there, their ordeal would not be over for they would still have to row across the wide stretch of open water that lay between themselves and the land. They were hardy men, though, long accustomed to hardship and deprivation, and the thought that they might not make it was far from their minds.

After thirty-five minutes of extremely hard going, his body and extremities numbed with the cold and his face so encased in snow and ice that he was almost unrecognizable, Arthur Batson slowed down. He was beginning to experience the first indications of exhaustion and hypothermia. The force of the raging elements on his scantily clad body had already begun to take its toll, and he was flagging badly. "Let's take a spell," he pleaded, "a minute or two, Bill, that's all I want."

"We can't," countered William, "it's too risky. It's getting worse by the minute and if we stop now we might be in trouble. I know you're tired, but we've got to try to keep going." Although he was considerably bigger and stronger than his brother, he was not in much better condition himself and for a brief moment or two had been tempted to do as Arthur had suggested. But the instincts that he had obeyed all his life now told him to press on.

Despite their best efforts, during the next half hour they were only able to cover a fraction of the distance back to the innermost edge of the ice-field. The gale-force wind buffeted them constantly and impeded their progress. Sometimes it stopped them dead in their tracks or even drove them backwards. Ice and snow coated them from head to foot, and at times they could see only mere inches ahead of them. While trying to cope with the extremely poor visibility, they also had to exercise extreme caution when picking their way over the treacherous ice beneath their feet. Bodies of clear water were beginning to open up all around them and the large ice-field had become a turbulent, shifting mass fraught with extreme danger. Overcompensating for the change in the wind, they had also unwittingly veered a considerable distance to the north. On several occasions they were confronted by ice rafted in layers so high that they had no alternative but to make long detours around them, which considerably added to the overall length of their homeward journey and caused them precious minutes that they could ill-afford to lose.

Finally, Arthur, shivering violently, his lungs burning,

his heart pounding in his chest, and barely able to take another breath, stopped again. "I've got to take a spell, Bill, b'y, I don't care what you say. Just for a little while, and then I'll be okay to go on again. You keep going if you want to. I'll catch up. Don't worry about me, I'll be okay."

William Batson, almost as exhausted as Arthur, knew that he could never leave his brother out there on the ice like that and, against his own better judgement, agreed to a short rest. Both men sat down on the ice where they had stopped. There was no semblance of shelter anywhere in the immediate vicinity where they could rest and minimize the brutal punishment to their faces and bodies. So they simply laid down and curled up on the ice and let the storm rage around them. Within a matter of a few seconds Arthur was asleep, unable to resist the overwhelming temptation to just close his eyes and let himself drift off. William, more alert to the danger of this and the possibility that if he did so he might never again wake up, forced himself to stay awake. As he lay there, he thought about Taffita at home, knowing that she would undoubtedly be starting to worry about him by now.

William then began to ponder the dire situation in which he and Arthur now found themselves. He had no idea how much distance they had covered, but figured that about an hour had elapsed since they had first set out on their arduous trek back to the punt. It seemed like an eternity, and he knew that he was slowly freezing to death and undoubtedly would do so if they didn't get there soon. He didn't realize it, but he and Arthur had also veered much farther to the north than they intended, and were now considerably off-course as well.

Ten minutes later William tried to prod the sleeping Arthur back to life so that they could resume their journey back to the punt. With the exception of a few painful moans and unintelligible mumbles, William's repeated efforts to get Arthur going again drew no response. He knew at that moment that his brother was in serious trouble. Finally, in desperation, he manhandled the nearly unconscious man to his feet and half-carried, half-dragged him for several minutes until Arthur, to William's immense relief, started stumbling along again on his own.

And then the unthinkable happened. One minute Arthur was there by his side – and then he was gone, swallowed by the body of water that had suddenly opened up on the very spot where he had been standing. William was stunned. His final fleeting glimpse of his brother was a sight that he could scarcely comprehend – one in which the only visible part of Arthur's submerged body was his upraised arm breaking the surface of the water as if trying to pull himself out – or in the act of saying goodbye.

A split second later, the ice beneath William's own feet parted and he too found himself thrown into the frigid water. As the weight of his clothes and boots pulled him down, something in the recesses of his numbed brain told him to push upward, to fight against the forces that were suffocating him and squeezing the life from his body – and without knowing how he got there, he found himself clinging to the ice at the edge of the open pool, too weak to pull himself out of the water. Each attempt to do so left him weaker and more exhausted, until finally all he wanted to do was let go and let himself sink into the waters of the bay – into oblivion and a quick, merciful death.

Still something within him wouldn't permit him to let go so easily, and finally, after several more attempts he somehow found the strength to pull himself up out of the water and onto the ice. By then all thoughts of continuing on to the punt were gone. His only desire now was to lie down where he was and go to sleep. He couldn't feel his feet, or his arms or legs, and the extreme shaking of his body threatened to push him back into the sea. He closed his eyes until the hypothermia that he had fought against for the last hour or more reached its final stage and a feeling of deep euphoria swept over him, bathing him in its serene, blissful warmth and comfort. Now, oblivious to the storm that still swirled around him, he closed his eyes in peace and contentment.

He wondered what was keeping Taffita and the children. He had the punt ready, the buckets and the tarpaulin were stored in the cuddy, and it was time for them to get started. If they didn't get underway soon, the Whites and the Baileys might get there before them and get the best of the birds-eggs and the berries. Why were they taking so long?

Ah, finally, he saw them coming, the children as usual shouting and jostling each other as they rushed along to be the first to the punt. And in the rear, with a basket in her arms that undoubtedly contained food and drink for their Sunday outing on Fox Island, came Taffita. Sweet, sweet Taffita. His eyes focused on her, and her alone, as she came closer and closer until finally only the fullness of her face was before him, flooding his intellect and his soul with the radiance of her smile. At that instant, the ice upon which he was lying opened once more and he joined his brother Arthur in the watery depths of the bay.

The bodies of William and Arthur Batson, among the first casualties of that fateful February day in Trinity Bay, were never recovered. In the days ahead, the two men would be counted among the long list of men classified as missing and presumed dead.

VI
Making for Shore

It was almost half past eleven by the time Bob and Charlie Bannister made it back to the edge of the ice-field and launched their punt into the water. A number of other boats that had been operating in the same general area had already pushed off and were starting to make their way back to shore. Fortunately, the Bannisters had stayed relatively close to each other after arriving there that morning and had not yet wandered any great distance out over the ice-field when the storm broke. They quickly realized, even though they were only about half a mile away from their punt, that they would have to abandon their search for seals and turn back. It was a prudent decision that enabled them to make their way back to the punt without too much difficulty. For once in his life, Charlie had acted with all due haste and hadn't held them up or caused any delay.

It was a good start, but now, before setting out for shore themselves, Bob Bannister had to make an important decision – one upon which his own safety and that of Charlie might very well depend. Should they try to head straight for home and hope that they could make English Head, or would they be carried too far south by the winds and the heavy tides to be able to negotiate their way around it? Might it be better to take a different tack altogether? He knew that if they could make it safely around English Head, the rest of the seven-mile journey back to Robinhood could then be made in the lee of the land and in less violent waters. And, if they had to, they could put in to English Harbour or Salmon Cove along the way. Still, he knew that it would take at least a couple of hours of hard rowing, possibly a lot longer, to do it. Their jib sail would be of no use to them either, for with the wind blowing hard out of the northeast on their forward right quarter, using the sail would undoubtedly only serve to carry them farther out into the bay and far wide of their mark.

The cliffs of the Horse Chops were only three and a half miles away. Heading there, however, would mean that they would have to row almost directly into the face of the gale-force wind. Still, it was only a third of the distance and temptingly close in the circumstances. The only other alternative was to try to head across Trinity Bay in the general direction of Bonaventure Head and Ireland's Eye. While this would permit them to make use of the jib sail, it would entail a significantly greater distance of some sixteen to twenty miles, depending on where they might eventually come ashore. The other danger, if they chose that option, was that they might miss these targets altogether. In that case they would probably be blown an additional eight to ten miles across the entire width of the bay in the direction of the string of communities stretching from Grates Cove to Heart's Content on the bay's far south side – or worse still, out into the open ocean.

There was no easy and obvious answer, but between the snow squalls, Bannister was able to determine that most of the other boats in his immediate vicinity seemed to be trying for the Horse Chops. He had already been leaning that way himself, and now the knowledge that so many others had elected to go in that direction cemented his decision.

"Take your oar, Charlie," he told his son, "and let's get

started. We'll try for Hay Cove.[6] We should be able to land there without too much trouble. We'll both have to row. That way we should be able to make better headway against the wind. Now, my son, get moving. The quicker we're out there, the sooner we'll be home – before your mother gets too worried about us."

Both he and Charlie had shed their warm jackets earlier before leaving the punt to search for seals, but now, before pushing off into the open waters of the bay, they retrieved them from the stern of the punt and put them back on again. To their dismay, however, they discovered that two of the four woolen cuffs that they had left there and both of their caps had disappeared, having undoubtedly been carried away by the wind.

Charlie, pulling on the two remaining cuffs, took his usual place at the left oar while his father settled himself onto the center tawt beside him. They had rowed together in this manner, father on the right and son on the left, for as long as they could remember, and now force of habit compelled them to assume their customary positions. It was a simple, automatic, unthinking action on the part of both men – but one that for Charlie would have grave consequences soon afterward.

Once launched, their tiny punt was no match for the angry sea. Only minutes after pushing away from the ice-field, they were already being tossed about violently by the ten to fifteen-foot waves that crashed all around them. One moment their small boat would be pointing almost straight upward as it rode the crest of an oncoming wave

---

[6] Hay Cove is a small semi-sheltered cove two miles north-east of English Head, one of the very few accessible spots in this stretch of rugged coastline.

and the next moment plummeting downward in its trough until it seemed as if they were descending into the very depths of the churning ocean itself. They found it extremely difficult to control the punt and keep it headed in the right direction. Already, sea-water was beginning to flood the bottom of the punt, forcing Bob to bail as he rowed, which was certainly no easy task in the tempest that swirled all around them.

"It will probably be a bit better when we get in closer to the land," Bob tried to reassure his son. He reasoned, or at least hoped, that as they got closer to the shore the howling northeast wind might deflect off the high cliffs of the Horse Chops and save its worse impact for farther out into the bay.

"And make sure that you hold onto that oar tight, Charlie," he added, "we don't want to lose one. If we do, we're finished."

"Don't worry, Da, I've got a good grip on it," Charlie assured him, "I'll be okay. You just look after yourself. Why don't you take one of these cuffs? It'll be better than neither one at all."

"No, my son, you keep them on for now. Perhaps I'll take a turn with them later on." At that moment his thoughts were only for the safety of his son and he would have willingly given him his jacket and everything else from his own body if he thought it would have made any difference to the boy's comfort and well-being.

Gradually the distance between themselves and the ice-field lengthened. It was painfully slow progress and they had to fight tooth and nail for every inch they made. Sometimes they were blown backwards a short distance and had to redouble their efforts to regain the lost yardage. After fifty minutes of the most arduous rowing that either of them had ever done in their lifetimes, they had managed to cover only a third of the distance to the shore.

Bannister thought about Flora at home. She would undoubtedly be very worried about him and Charlie by now and watching for them from the kitchen window. Having lost a brother to the sea many years earlier and witnessing on many other occasions the havoc that it could wreak upon communities and their people, she hated and feared the sea with great passion. Every time Bob or any of her sons left to go out on the salt water in their boats, she silently pleaded with God to watch over them and bring them safely back home again. No matter how calm the day or how still the waters of the bay, she always admitted that the knot in her stomach never went away until she finally saw their punt heave back into view in the cove. She could only shed her feeling of uneasiness when she knew that they were all safely back on shore.

Bob Bannister was also worried about his other two sons, John and Job. He hadn't seen or spoken to either of them during the past two days and he didn't know if they had gone out to the ice-field that morning or not. He prayed fervently that they had chosen to stay at home but knew in his heart that in all likelihood they too had gone out with all the others. His primary concern at the moment, though, was getting Charlie safely to land.

The fury of the sea, as Bannister had hoped, subsided somewhat as they got closer to shore, which gave both of them some relief and renewed optimism. But then, to their consternation, they began to experience yet another problem. With the continuing sharp drop in the temperature, the spray coming in over the punt with each oncoming wave now froze wherever it hit and covered their bodies.

Within the space of the next fifteen or twenty minutes it also coated their tiny boat in a layer of ice that was inches thick in some places, particularly on Charlie's side of the fragile craft. It was a condition that made the punt very vulnerable to swamping and capsizing. Bannister attempted to chip some of it away with his oar, but each time he took the oar out of the water to do so, he lost valuable ground and the punt careened wildly off course and spun out of control. He quickly concluded that there was nothing to do but to ignore the ice build-up and simply row on and take their chances.

For another twenty minutes they fought their way toward the shore. The punt, now badly out of trim and totally covered with ice, was beginning to wallow dangerously in the water under the additional weight. Nevertheless, they continued to make slow but steady progress. They were, however, still at least a mile and a half from shore, and their strength and endurance were rapidly waning.

It was at that point that Bob Bannister heard his son tell him, "Da, I think I'm freezing." Charlie's words were strangely garbled and he had difficulty getting them out. His body was numbed despite the heavy jacket that he was wearing and the fact that he had been continuously rowing into the teeth of the gale for an hour and forty-five minutes. He couldn't feel his feet, he had lost all feeling in his ears, and the woolen cuffs on his hands were literally frozen to the oar. It was the first time the normally talkative boy had spoken in more than thirty minutes.

Bannister, who had been totally preoccupied with his own share of the rowing, the bailing, and the constant struggle to keep the punt headed in the right direction, glanced sideways at his son for one of the few times since leaving the ice-field. He was horrified by what he saw.

Charlie, rowing in the left oar position, had been taking the full brunt of the freezing spray on the more exposed side of the punt for the last half hour or more. His entire body was encased in ice and his rowing movements were becoming jerkier and more feeble by the minute. Every stroke was now an obvious ordeal. The hair of his uncovered head was frozen into grotesque strands that stood off wildly in every direction like icicles. Long slivers of ice extended downward from his eyebrows, his nose and mouth, and his chin. The ice virtually cemented his head and face to his upper chest area. He was unrecognizable. Bannister suddenly realized that he himself had been sheltered by his son's body from the worst of the spray coming in over the exposed side of the punt. He could scarcely comprehend that something as horrific as this could have happened to Charlie in such a short time – and his first thought was that he himself was to blame. How could he have sat next to his son on the tawt all that while and not even been aware of what was happening to him?

Although they were still an agonizingly long way from the safety of Hay Cove, he had no choice but to stop rowing and try to do whatever he could for his son. As the punt pitched wildly on its own, he gingerly picked as much of the ice away from Charlie's head, face, and body as he could without hurting him any further, talking to him continuously as he did so.

"Don't worry, Charlie, you'll be okay. We're getting close to shore now. You just take a spell and I'll do the rowing from here on in. I didn't know. Why didn't you say something?"

The boy groaned in response, but otherwise showed no reaction to his father's efforts to help him. Bannister knew that he had to get Charlie off the tawt and down to the bottom of the punt, and somehow shelter him from the continuing freezing spray. He had no choice, even though several inches of icy water still covered the bottom of the boat despite his constant bailing. Almost without thinking he reached for the jib sail and laid it over the floor-boards at his feet, with the short mast of the little sail extending out over the stern of the boat. He then lifted Charlie down upon the canvas as best he could while trying desperately to keep both of them from falling overboard into the sea. With a heavy heart, he folded the slack of the canvas over Charlie's frozen body to cover as much of it as possible. It was the best he could do in the circumstances.

By now they had drifted a considerable distance south of their destination. It took all of Bannister's strength to get the punt moving again and pointed in the right direction. Ignoring his own extreme discomfort and exhaustion, his only thought now was to get Charlie to the safety of the land before the boy perished. Bannister's lungs were bursting, his arms felt like lead weights, and his fingers, like Charlie's, were almost frozen in place where they gripped the oars. Still he rowed on, his eyes alternating between the pounding sea and the outline of his son's freezing body lying under the canvas in front of him. His mind was as numbed as his own frozen body and he had lost all track of time. He rowed by instinct only, without conscious thought or effort, until finally the punt butted roughly up against the rocks on the shore of Hay Cove. He slumped forward on the oars to try to revive himself before getting out. It had been almost three hours since they had pushed off from the ice-field.

VII
Running with the Storm

Bill Day, faced with the same decision as Bob Bannister, quickly made up his mind that he and his cousin, Charles Day, would also head for the Horse Chops since it was the nearest point of land. As usual, he did not bother to ask his partner what his thoughts were on the matter. Unlike the Bannisters, however, the Days had been a considerable distance out on the ice-field when the storm came upon them, and were therefore much later in getting back to their punt and launching it into the water. By the time they were ready to pull away, the strength of the wind had already reached gale force and the intensity of the storm was approaching its zenith. The temperature, which was already well below the freezing point, also continued to plummet.

Two other men from Salmon Cove, George Ivany and Edward Pottle, who happened to be hunting seals nearby, left at the same time in their own seventeen-foot punt. Several other boats were already in the water and making for shore while still others were in the process of being made ready for the bolt to the land. In the chaotic rush for shore, most of the larger four-oared punts, with their extra manpower and greater oar capacity, were able to quickly outdistance their smaller two-oared counterparts and thus get a bit closer to the land before the storm reached its full height.

The large twenty-one foot, four-oared punt of the Days, however, held little advantage for them in their own situation. Because of its size and greater weight, and with only the two of them to row it, it would undoubtedly be very difficult to keep it moving into the wind. The one edge that it did have over the smaller punts was that it was a bit more stable in rough water.

The rowing was grueling right from the start, even for the powerfully built Day. His partner occupied the forward tawt while he positioned himself on the rear one. They each wielded a pair of oars. Charles, because he was closest to the dill,[7] was also the one who had to do the bailing, for water had begun to build up in the bottom of the punt as soon as they pushed off from the ice-field. Unlike the majority of the other men who happened to be caught out in the bay at the time, both Bill and Charles Day had had the good sense to put their heavy jackets and caps back on when it had become obvious that bad weather was approaching. Thus, they were dressed as well as they could possibly have been in the circumstances for the dash for home.

An agreement had been made with Ivany and Pottle before leaving the ice that the two punts would try to stay as close as possible to each other on their homeward journey in case either had to be abandoned along the way. Since they would be heading almost directly into the wind, the use of their jib sails would be pointless. They, like the Bannisters, would have only their oars to rely on to get them home. Also, because they had landed their punts about a mile farther south than the Bannisters when they had first arrived at the ice-field that morning, they would now have to cover a much longer distance before reaching

---

[7] The space under a boat's floor-boards where bilge water collects, and from where its bailed out.

the Horse Chops.

The two punts kept as close to each other as the wind and the turbulence of the sea would permit. At times they were practically side by side and at other times as much as a hundred feet apart, but always within sight and hailing distance of each other. They were, unfortunately, making pitifully slow progress, and after an hour of strenuous rowing both boats had covered less than a mile since leaving the ice-pack. Despite their best efforts to stay on course, they were gradually being forced south of their destination and out into the bay. The ice build-up from the driving spray was also making the punts top-heavy and difficult to manoeuver. Bill and Charles Day, as well as Ivany and Pottle in the other punt, had to interrupt their rowing constantly to use their oars to chip the fast-forming ice off, in order to maintain at least some semblance of trim and stability. The freezing spray also coated their bodies and clothing which further inhibited their ability to row as efficiently as they normally did.

In the extremely poor visibility, Bill Day had no way of telling with any certainty how far they had come. After what he judged to be another hour or more, it was obvious that they were still not much farther ahead. He concluded then that their attempt to reach the Horse Chops would be futile and that they would have to try for somewhere else. After two hours of continuous hard rowing they had only managed to cover a fraction of the distance to the shore and were losing ground by the minute. Again, without bothering to consult with Charles, Bill Day made another arbitrary decision. He hailed Ivany and Pottle, and inside of a few minutes the two boats were within shouting distance of each other.

"This is no good, George, b'y," he bellowed to make

himself heard across the small open space that now separated the two punts. "We'll never make it this way. We'll perish long before we reach land, either drown or freeze to death."

"What do you think we should do then?" Ivany shouted back.

"Put up our jibs and head for Bonaventure. I think that's our best bet. I know it's a long distance, but I can't see any other way. Can you think of anything better?"

Ivany considered carefully before committing himself, then reluctantly conceded. "No. I suppose you're right," he finally replied, "but let me and Edward go on ahead of you a bit so you can keep an eye on us. This old thing is as cranky[8] as the devil when the sail is up."

"All right, but try to stay close. Our chances will be a lot better if we stay together."

This conversation and the decision to change their course had taken place without any input from either Charles Day or Edward Pottle. Neither of these men, however, would have raised any objection for they too were in full agreement with Bill Day's assessment. So in each punt the jib sail was erected with its guide rope tied down in place to enable the embattled occupants to continue their rowing and to use their oars to guide and steer the two boats toward their new destination.

With the wind now in their backs, the going immediately became much easier and the four men were able to slacken their efforts a little and let the wind and their sails carry them along. Although its impact had lessened

---

[8] The term generally applied to boats which because of poor craftsmanship or design flaws are more susceptable to overturning or capsizing than most other boats of their type.

somewhat because they were no longer butting against the gale, the freezing spray coming in over the sides nevertheless remained a problem. It continued to add to their discomfort and to the already thick ice build-up on the punt, so much so that they still couldn't let their guard down. They knew they would have to continue chipping it away as best they could. Their greatest concern now, though, was to prevent their tiny boats from being swamped by following waves that threatened to overtake them as they yawed and lurched in the wake of the previous ones. It required their full concentration and seamanship to counteract this new and equally deadly danger.

The four men were settled in for what they knew would be a long and extremely dangerous flight up the bay. Both boats continued to ice up badly and take on water, and their occupants were wet, tired, and chilled to the bone – and still a very long way from the safety of the land. Their visibility was extremely limited, at times non-existent, preventing them from seeing more than a couple of hundred feet in any direction. Sometimes they lost sight of each other altogether for short periods of time. At no time were they able to see the shoreline on their starboard side. They were forced to rely totally on their own innate sense of direction to keep them pointed toward their intended destination. Bill Day was worried that the wind might shift even more northerly or northwesterly without them realizing it and carry them out of the bay altogether and out into the open Atlantic Ocean. If that happened, they would have no chance of surviving at all.

An hour into their new course up the bay, Day was suddenly alarmed to see that the punt in which Ivany and Pottle were travelling was beginning to behave very erratically. His concern increased each time he saw the other boat heel over on its side until it seemed that the mast and sail were almost touching the water while Ivany and Pottle frantically shifted their weight to the other side of the punt to try to prevent it from tipping over and capsizing. Day knew that his friends would never make it all the way to Bonaventure in that condition, and that the imperilled punt was likely to go under at any minute. He thought to himself, "George was right, that devilin' old skow is the crankiest thing in the bay. And now with all that ice on her, she's gotten even worse. He should have had the sense to put a hole in her and sink the jinker in the bay a long time ago."

Ivany and Pottle were so preoccupied with their frantic efforts to stave off imminent disaster that several minutes elapsed before they finally took notice of Day's frenzied motions to take down the sail and let them come alongside. Day had quickly come to the conclusion that their only option now was to abandon the smaller boat and for the other two men to transfer themselves to his punt for the rest of the journey.

In the mountainous sea, getting Ivany and Pottle from their own boat and into the other was no easy matter, and it took the combined strength, seamanship, and ingenuity of all four men to get the two punts broadside with each other and steadied long enough to make the transfer. When they had done so, they released the other boat and watched it spin away on the waves. The jib sail on the Days' boat was then put up again, and they proceeded on their way. In the now crowded remaining boat, with Ivany crouched in the bow trying to scan ahead for ice pans and other chunks of floating ice, Bill and Charles Day resumed their original rowing positions. Pottle, who had gotten soaked to the skin during the transfer, settled himself on the tawt beside Charles to help with the rowing, and to try to coax some life back into his wet and chilled body.

Ten minutes later the punt in which the four of them were now travelling almost capsized when it was caught broadside by a large wave that broke over them before they could take measures to avoid it. Only their frantic last-second maneuvering and timely bailing prevented the boat, its nose buried in the sea and taking on a great amount of water, from swamping. Ivany, in the bow, had almost been swept overboard. He was saved only because he had had the presence of mind and the quickness of body to grab the gunnel and hold on for dear life as the incoming water rushed over him. It had been a close call and all four men were shaken by it. All feared that this was likely to happen again and again.

Once more Bill Day took charge, "We're too high in the water," he told the others. "We're top heavy. George, you're going to have to croop down lower. And you, Ed, are going to have to give your oar back to Charles and lie down on the floorboards there between me and him. There's nothing else to do, or we'll be capsized for sure the next time."

The other men, accepting the truth and wisdom of Day's words, did as he ordered. Extremely cold and in great discomfort, they continued on. Their four and a half hour battle with the storm, two hours of which had been spent in their initial futile attempt to reach the Horse Chops, had left them weakened and exhausted. They did not know where they were, only that they were still hopefully somewhere within the confines of Trinity Bay. They had no way of telling how far they had come or how much distance still lay between themselves and the safety of the shore. On several subsequent occasions, larger than usual waves sweeping in unexpectedly on their windward side threatened to swamp them, forcing them again and again to take quick evasive action to avert disaster.

Charles Day, who had uttered scarcely a word since leaving the ice-field, was at that point feeling the onset of hypothermia. He was shivering violently and was rapidly losing all sense of feeling in his limbs and extremities. Finally he spoke up, "Bill, I think I'm giving out. I don't think I can keep rowing much longer. I just haven't got the strength."

Bill Day had always heard that a man's best chance of surviving if caught out in dire weather conditions like this was to try to keep moving as long as possible to keep the blood circulating and the heart beating – and now, firm in this conviction, he encouraged his young partner to keep rowing. It was what he himself would do in the circumstances. It was perhaps misguided advice and may have in fact been the worst thing for Charles to do in his weakened state. But Day firmly believed that if Charles stopped now and did nothing for the rest of the journey, he might never make it to shore alive. Day, also cognizant of the extreme risk of trying to rearrange their order in the small punt while it continued to pitch and buck wildly in the raging sea, decided against trying to have the other men exchange positions.

Edward Pottle was also by then in serious trouble. His body too was now shaking violently, his vision blurred, his body numbed, and he was oblivious to most of what was going on around him. He was, in fact, even worse off than Charles Day, for he was already in an advanced state of extreme cold and utter exhaustion. Worse still, he was literally frozen to the floorboards of the punt. Bill Day's repeated attempts to communicate with him and to try to reassure him that they would soon reach land drew only an occasional moan, and Day knew that Pottle couldn't last much longer in his present condition.

He hadn't heard anything from George Ivany in quite some time either. Because he was facing toward the stern in order to row, he couldn't see Ivany without looking back over his shoulder. A quick glance now told him that Ivany had snuggled down in the bow of the punt to shelter himself as best he could from the storm. But he couldn't tell if Ivany was conscious or not. The fact that Ivany didn't respond to his shouted questions worried him, and he wondered if Ivany, like Pottle, might be in trouble. Day realized that he himself was now the only man on board alert and with any strength left – and that he was beginning to wane rapidly.

Another fifteen minutes saw the condition of all four men deteriorate further still. Slammed by icy blasts of wind, driving snow, and freezing spray, they were slowly freezing to death in the abysmally low temperature. It was at that moment that Day heard Charles behind him groan loudly and say, "Oh, Bill." Turning around, he saw to his disbelief that the oars were missing from Charles' hands, yet Charles, oblivious to their disappearance, continued to move his arms and body in an automatic rowing motion. Day knew at that moment that his cousin was very near death, and indeed a few minutes later the young man pitched forward and fell on top of the prostrate body of Pottle in the bottom of the boat.

With the reality of Charles' condition finally sunk in, Bill Day pleaded with his cousin to hold on. "Just a little longer, Charl," he begged. "I'm sure we're getting close to the land. I'll get you ashore somehow and look after you.

Just stay alive 'til I do. You can do it."

But his pleas were in vain, for Charles was already dead. Day, the only one now left to row, had no choice but to try to carry on by himself. There was nothing he could do for Charles, or for Edward Pottle or George Ivany either for that matter. He alone was left to get them to shore. And then, to his immense surprise, he heard Ivany, who he had assumed by now was unconscious, or perhaps even dead, shout, "I see the land!"

Through the driving snow, Day recognized the point of land that Ivany had spotted as Bonaventure Head, but he knew that they had drifted too far south of it to be able to turn around and put in there. His flagging spirits, nevertheless, were buoyed because he knew that Ireland's Eye lay dead ahead, only a few miles farther along. Then, incredulously, he heard Pottle ask, "Are we near land yet?" They were the very last words that Edward Pottle would ever utter, for a few minutes later he too expired. With two dead men in the boat, and himself and Ivany on the verge of collapse, Bill Day steered for Ireland's Eye.

VIII
Waiting on Shore

At half past five that Saturday morning, William Nurse was at the kitchen table of his son George's house in Salmon Cove eating his breakfast as he listened to George telling him about his plans for the day. From long custom, the old man had already been up for an hour or more, sitting there in the darkness of the house and looking out toward the bay, waiting for the sun to rise. It looked like it was going to be a good day.

William's fragile body, bent and twisted by extremely severe and painful arthritis brought on by years of toil and exposure to the worst that the elements had to offer, made him a much older man than his sixty-nine years would otherwise suggest. Every step he took was a painful endeavour, yet he bore the pain stoically and tried to keep going, giving up only when it was too unbearable to carry on, making it necessary for him to sit or lie down for a while.

He was a widower. His first wife, Arianna, had died two years after giving birth to their first child, George. William remarried two years later and his second wife, Celia, bore him three more sons, Henry, Charles, and William Jr. (Billy), before she too passed way. She also bore him a daughter whom he christened Arianna after his first wife. After Henry and Charles were old enough to marry and move out into their own homes, Billy left as well to live with his brother George. This was a move of convenience to accommodate Billy's joining George as a junior fishing partner, leaving only Nurse and his daughter to continue to live in the old two-story house in which he had been born and in which he and his two wives had spent their entire married lives.

For the first two years he and young Arianna managed quite well on their own and he had given his family no cause to worry about him. By the third year, however, they noticed that he was beginning to experience increasingly frequent periods of forgetfulness and absent-mindedness. He was becoming what the people of the area called "a bit low-minded," their term for his increasing bouts of confusion and forgetfulness. Mildly concerned at first, his family had watched as his mental condition gradually worsened in the ensuing months until George, afraid that the old man might do himself harm or burn the house down, came to him one day and told him, "Father, you and Arianna are coming to live with me and Mary Anne, that's all there is to it. So get your clothes and your kit together, and whatever else you and Arianna want to take with you, and come on back with me."

Although it was an act steeped in love and compassion for his father, George had expected the old man to balk at the idea. Surprisingly, his father had raised no objections. Perhaps he had expected George to come for him, or, having spent so many cold and lonely nights in the old house, had even welcomed it. He meekly surrendered his independence and moved in with George and his family that same day. From that day forward, William Nurse's four sons took their ailing father under their wing and did their very best to treat him with the dignity and respect that he deserved. They and their wives and their children encircled him with their love and affection and looked after him as best they could, and continued to make him an important and central part of their everyday lives.

As time passed, William's mental condition continued to worsen, slowly deteriorating further until eventually most of his waking hours were spent in the fuzzy, far-away world into which he had now retreated. Interspersed with his "low-mindedness" were short, intermittent periods of normality during which his mind was clear and his memory as good as it had ever been. In his more lucid moments, he was fully aware of everything going on around him, could carry on normal conversations with other people, and was quite capable of looking after himself.

Others in the community had by that time taken it upon themselves to look out for him also. Whenever he appeared to be confused or seemed to be wandering aimlessly, they led him home, even though that might be only a few houses away. If he showed up down around the wharves and the fishing stages, someone made sure that he didn't do anything dangerous, and when he knocked on their doors to tell them that he was thirsty or hungry they gave him food and drink. Mary Barnes, who lived in the last house on the path leading to English Harbour, always kept a vigilant eye out for him to make sure he didn't stray outside the confines of the community. Cyril Fifield did likewise on the other side to make sure that he didn't wander off beyond the boundaries of Salmon Cove in the direction of Robinhood and Ship Cove. William Nurse's family, not wishing to confine him or restrict his freedom, were very grateful for the concern and help of the other residents of the community.

That morning, as he sat at the kitchen table, Nurse was enjoying one of his more lucid moments, and listened with interest and understanding as his son, George, told him, "Skipper, me and the boys are going out for a few swiles this morning. The ice is in and we heard there's lots of them out there. It looks like a wonderful day for it, too."

The "boys" he was referring to were his brothers, Henry, Charles, and Billy, all fully grown men now.

"I think we're going to take the big punt this time. Better for us to be all together," George told his father, adding, "how would you like a good feed of flippers for your supper tonight, Old Man? Make your mouth water, wouldn't it?"

Nurse nodded his agreement. He wished that he were able to go out himself, but knew that his days out on the water were long past. Sadly, now all he could do was watch others come and go. Sometimes he could remember exactly how it had been when he was young and fit. His family had always been at the core of his existence and he had toiled long and hard to keep them fed and to make sure that they always had a roof over their heads and a bed to lie in. He had slowly destroyed his once strong body in the process. When he sometimes thought about it, he was satisfied that he had done his best to raise his four sons to be God-fearing men of integrity, and to be as hard-working and as industrious as himself. He took it as his due that it was now their turn to look after him. While he now lived with George, the oldest, he was sure that any of the others would have gladly taken him into their homes and looked after him equally well for the rest of his days. This morning, as he listened to George, he silently thanked God for having given him four such wonderful boys.

His sons were all strong, brawny men who had thus far given him eight grandchildren, an equal number of girls and boys. The four brothers had many things in common – fishing together as a crew, providing well for their families (with the exception of Billy who was not yet married), and attending Church regularly. Although they often quarreled and bickered with each other, as brothers often do, they got along very well in their work and in their daily interactions.

Yet they were all different. George, as befitted the eldest, was the sensible one. He was the one to whom the rest of the clan took their troubles and their difficulties. He was now forty-two years of age, fifteen years older than Henry, the next in line, and the others all trusted implicitly in his counsel and advice. Whenever anything of a serious nature had to be dealt with within the family, he was usually the one to whom they looked for guidance and direction.

Henry, always shy and reserved, was the most gifted of the lot. His hands, although calloused and rough from fishing, were capable of transforming even the crudest piece of wood into a work of art. Some of the handiwork that adorned the interior of St. Nicholas' Church in Salmon Cove was the product of his labours, along with much of the furniture in the community that he had built for other people during the non-fishing winter months.

Charles was the musical one, a fine self-taught musician. He and his fiddle were pressed into service every time the people of the community packed the hall or the school for wedding receptions, soirees, concerts, or other festive occasions. His occasional visits to the homes of relatives and friends throughout Trinity Bight invariably ended up as toe-tapping, hand-clapping affairs that usually lasted well into the wee hours of the morning. A quiet, soft-spoken man, he was usually contented to let his fiddle music do most of the talking for him.

Billy, age 20, was the live wire and the ladies man. By the time he was eighteen, he had left a trail of broken hearts from Bonaventure Head to Port Union (and a child or two it was suspected), and was one of the most sought after young men in the Bight. Having escaped the matrimonial trap thus far, he had no intentions of settling down anytime in the foreseeable future unless one of his many conquests eventually happened to catch up with him. The single life was, for him, much too good and too varied to be surrendered lightly.

As his four sons were departing for the ice that morning, William Nurse felt that he had been sitting around long enough in the kitchen and thought that he too should be out and about. After leaving the house, he stopped for a few minutes to watch the convoy of punts making its way out to the ice-field. Forgetting for the moment that George had told him that they were all going out swiling that morning, he wondered what so many of them were doing out there and where they were all going. At nine-thirty a.m., after poking about the community for almost two hours, he took off his coat. He felt too hot and uncomfortable in the warm morning air, his legs were starting to ache, and he needed a drink of water.

At eleven a.m., after leaving the house of John Barnes, where he had stopped and spent the best part of an hour, he put his coat back on. He was suddenly chilled by a sharp gust of cold wind from the north-east that cut through his slight inner clothing. Stopping once more, this time to size up the ominous black clouds approaching from the north-east, a shudder passed through his body and he experienced a momentary feeling of unease – before quickly retreating once again into his own, comfortable inner world and proceeding on his way. After walking a short distance, he met George's wife, Mary Anne, who had come looking for him to bring him home for his mid-day meal. Tucking her arm in his, she led him back to the house.

At three-thirty that afternoon, this time from the vantage point of his son's kitchen window, he looked out upon the bay once more, seeing through the driving snow and his still befuddled mind, glimpses of the sea that now roiled and raged turbulently before his eyes. For the second time that day, a sense of foreboding swept over him. It caused him to avert his eyes and focus them on the cup of hot tea that his daughter-in-law had just set down on the table for him. This time he couldn't shake the feeling of unease and decided he would go outside again for a few minutes. When he stepped around the corner of the house, a blast of wind hit him full on. He changed his mind yet again and turned around and went back into the house where he took up his usual spot at the kitchen table.

Although he had no way of knowing it, it was at that very moment that his four sons were drowning out in the bay, only two and a half miles from where he was sitting. They had been making good progress toward shore when their ice-covered punt was smashed by a crashing wave that caught it broadside and capsized it – leaving George, Henry, Charles, and Billy Nurse to perish in the bay.

IX
Out on the Chops

The four Nurse brothers had drowned in the bay at approximately three-thirty on Saturday afternoon, February 27th, 1892. Several hours before this, however, many other men on shore were already becoming uneasy and apprehensive about the change in the weather and its consequences for the men and boys who had gone out swiling. One of these was John Butler, who had been walking the cliffs of the Horse Chops since mid-day, hoping to be able to detect the presence of punts making their way in from the ice-field. Earlier that morning, he and Mary and their four children had wended their way on foot from Ship Cove to English Harbour for the burial of his brother-in-law, Joseph Penny. While the funeral service wouldn't be held until two o'clock that afternoon, the immediate family and close relatives, as was the usual custom, congregated well ahead of time in the house of the deceased for the final hours of his wake and the offering of family prayers before leaving for the Church.

At one point in the morning, Butler experienced a foreboding sense of gloom which at the time he attributed to his brother-in-law's death, or to the fact that in all these years he had never really tried to be on good terms with Joe Penny, and now it was too late. He would recall that feeling later and realize that it had nothing at all to do with Penny, but had been a premonition of the terrible events that would unfold later that day. This feeling of disquiet, and the heat and the confusion of the crowded house, prompted him to leave with the intention of taking a short walk around the harbour by himself.

"You make sure you're not gone too long now," his caustic wife cautioned him before he left. "If I know you, John, you're just as likely to go wandering off somewhere by yourself and lose all track of time, and be late for poor Joe's funeral."

Assuring her that he would only be gone a short while, he started out on his walk. As he did so, he took note of the sharp drop in the temperature and the dark storm clouds looming on the horizon. Although it was still a relatively good day, he felt that the exceptionally fine weather of the morning was in for a turn. By eleven o'clock, as the wind picked up and veered northeasterly, snow began to fall and he became a bit concerned, hoping that his brother, Alexander, and his nephew, Jimmy, would have the good sense to come in from the ice soon, whether they had killed any seals or not. If they stayed out much longer, they might have a very difficult time of it rowing back in.

By twelve noon, as the storm intensified, Butler's growing apprehension had increased to the point of outright worry, and he left English Harbour to go to the Horse Chops where he hoped he might get a good view of the bay and whatever was happening out there. He had walked about two miles along the footpath that led to the Horse Chops, some five miles distant, when he met two other men, Robert Penny and Robert Ivany, coming towards him from the opposite direction. Both men were from English Harbour. They too had been worried about their brothers and other family members out in the bay, and had gone out on the Horse Chops to see if they could spot them coming in.

"See anything?" Butler queried.

"Not a thing," replied Penny, "Can't see out no distance at all with the snow blowing like it is. I wouldn't say it's too good for the poor devils out there on the water right now, though. I certainly wouldn't want to be out there myself, that's for sure."

The snow, now much heavier and driven by winds that had already reached gale force, had all but obliterated any view of the open bay, permitting them only an occasional glimpse of a second or two duration between squalls.

"There's not much point staying out here like this," added Ivany, "I'm going back. I'm freezing and I'm starved. I haven't had a bite to eat yet today, and I got to get washed and shaved and ready for Joe's funeral. I suppose they'll all be okay."

The last thing that John Butler intended to do at that moment was leave and go back. All thought of his brother-in-law's funeral had been pushed from his head, and his mind was now fully preoccupied with the thought of Alexander and Jimmy and the others out in the bay. In the space of the next few minutes, he was able to persuade both Penny and Ivany to stay out there with him for a while longer. "It might clear up a bit and we'll be able to see better," he told them, "we'll have plenty of time to go back and get ready for the funeral."

"But I got to get myself warmed up first," Penny replied, "If I'm going to be out here a while, we got to get a good fire going somewhere because I'm just about frozen to death."

The three men retraced their steps about a quarter of a mile to a spot directly overlooking Hay Cove. There they chose a sheltered place on the top of the cliffs where they gathered dry brush, boughs, and moldow[9] from the stunted spruce of the area and tried to make a fire. It was no easy matter in the high wind but after several

[9] Lichen from spruce trees.

unsuccessful attempts, they finally managed to get it started. While Penny and Ivany sat next to the fire trying to restore warmth to their cold bodies, Butler continued to rummage around for additional dry wood and brush to keep replenishing the fire whenever it burned down too low. For the next two hours, as the wind and the snow increased in intensity, the three men stayed by the fire – talking, smoking, and trying to keep themselves warm. Every ten or fifteen minutes, one of them would rise and walk back out on the path a short distance to check the bay.

By this time they were all convinced that the men out in the bay were in serious trouble. Butler, Ivany, and Penny had all decided that they would now stay out there as long as possible. Joe Penny's funeral would just have to go ahead without them. Their decision to remain where they were was based on the knowledge that this would probably be the closest point of land for most of the men leaving the ice-field and that, even though they would have to pull against the high head-wind, it was the spot towards which most of them would undoubtedly steer.

Another half hour passed and the three men, despite the fire, were themselves feeling very cold and uncomfortable. As well, Butler was so anxious now that he could no longer stay still. Briskly clapping his arms to his chest and shoulders to stave off the bitter bite of the wind, while taking care to protect his injured fingers, he left once more to check out into the bay. This time the driving snow abated for a few seconds – just long enough for him to be sure that he had spotted a punt not far off from the land. He waited for another momentary break in the snow to enable him to see out into the water again.

"By Jove!" he exclaimed to himself. "That's Henry George Batson's punt, I know it is."

The punt, with Batson and two other men in it whom he couldn't recognize from where he stood, was only a few hundred yards off from the shore. Yet Butler could see that they were having great difficulty covering the short distance that still stood between themselves and the land.

"They're so iced up they can hardly row," he thought to himself, "They must be frozen. If they don't get in soon they'll surely perish."

Retracing his steps a short distance, he called out to Ivany and Penny. "B'ys, come quick. Henry George Batson is on the way in with two others, and it looks like they're having trouble."

When Penny and Ivany rejoined him, they had to wait a few more minutes before he could point out the approaching men to them through a break in the snow squalls.

"Let's go down and meet them," said Penny, stating the obvious. Then the men made their way down over the steep hundred-foot embankment and gained a better view of the cove below. In doing so, they discovered to their amazement that directly beneath them several other punts and a number of men were already in on the beach. They had no way of knowing how long the men had been there, but they could immediately tell that most of them were so cold and exhausted by the ordeal of rowing in from the ice-field that they didn't have enough strength left to attempt to scale the cliffs where they had landed. Many of them were still sitting in their punts. A few had made it partway up the embankment, including, to Butler's immense relief, his brother Alexander and his nephew, Jimmy. Alexander also appeared to be trying to help another man whom John Butler recognized as William Stockley. Butler scrambled to their aid while Penny and Ivany went to help some of the others.

"My God, Alex, are you alright?" Butler's voice reflected the grave concern that he felt for his brother, "And what about Jimmy?"

Alexander, his face and body virtually encased in ice, had great difficulty speaking. "I'm okay, but I think my hands are frozen. I had to give my cuffs to Jimmy. Can you try to get him up on the path. I don't think I can carry him any farther."

"Don't worry, I'll get him up. You stay here and rest and keep an eye on Bill, and I'll be back down for you as soon as I get Jimmy settled away up top." John Butler then, despite the pain to his injured hand, picked up his semi-conscious nephew, settled him as best he could on his back and shoulders, and began the hard climb up to the path above. He spoke continually to the boy as they progressed upward, trying to reassure him that he was now safe. "We got a big fire going up there, Jimmy, and before you know it you'll be nice and warm and dry again. You'll be as good as new." He couldn't tell whether the boy had heard what he said or not.

When he had Jimmy settled away by the fire and had piled a few layers of boughs and brush over him for additional warmth and protection, he went back down for Alexander, who by this time, despite John's instructions to stay where he was and wait for him, had already made his own way almost to the top of the cliff. John led his brother the rest of the way back to the fire and settled him away on the ground beside his son. With both Alexander and Jimmy now as safe and secure as he could make them for the time being, John Butler went down to the beach below for the third time to check on Bill Stockley. But to his shock and dismay, he realized that in the brief time that had elapsed while he had been getting Alexander and

Jimmy up to the fire, the sixty-two-year-old Stockley had died. He had made it all the way to the shore only to expire on the beach shortly after reaching it.

Knowing that there was nothing more that he could now do for Stockley, he turned his attention to the others. He spotted Bob Bannister, still sitting in his punt. As Bannister's punt continued to grate on the spot where it had come ashore, Bob himself, virtually encased in ice, remained slumped over his oars in an apparent state of unconsciousness and his son was nowhere to be seen. When Butler was finally able to shake him awake, Bannister's first words were, "See to poor Charlie, will you? He's lying down in the punt. If we don't get him home soon, I expect he'll freeze to death."

Butler felt a sudden surge of pity on seeing the plight and anguish of his best friend and life-long companion. Butler pulled back the canvas and saw the boy's frozen body, and he knew immediately that it was too late for Charlie. He was already dead.

Trying very hard to keep his own emotions in check, he turned his attention back to Bannister and told him as gently as he could, "Bob, there's nothing to be done for Charlie now. He's gone. I'm sorry, but all I can do now is try to get you up out of here and thawed out before you perish yourself."

Bannister's heartrending cry cut through Butler like a knife. "No, that can't be right. He was alright when I laid him down there. Oh my oh my oh my, what can I do?" he wailed, "It's all my fault. It's all my fault. Oh God forgive me, what can I do?"

Several minutes passed before Butler was finally able to convince Bannister to get out of the punt and try to save himself before he too died. Only after agreeing to Butler's offer to remove Charlie's body from the punt and place it in a safer location farther up the cliff, did Bannister allow himself to be led away. With Butler at his side to help him get up to the path, the distraught man moaned over and over, "How will I ever be able to tell his mother? What will she think? How will she ever be able to forgive me for what I've done?"

As it turned out, he wouldn't have to be the one to tell her about Charlie's death after all. For a few minutes later, only halfway up the cliff, he himself died. He groaned and fell to the ground before Butler could catch him, and passed away on his hands and knees. The enormous strain of his three hour row to shore and the shock of Charlie's death – and the knowledge that it had been his fault, albeit unwittingly – had been too much for him. John Butler was heard to say to several people afterward that Bob Bannister had been so distraught that it seemed as if his heart had simply exploded in his chest.

In the meantime, Robert Penny had gone to the aid of a man whom he recognized as Thomas Butler, of Robinhood. He, like Bob Bannister, was still sitting over his oars in his punt. In the bottom of the boat with him were the frozen bodies of his eighteen-year-old son, Isaac, and James Penny of English Harbour, both of whom had perished before reaching the land. It was clear that Thomas himself was not far from death. It took Penny almost twenty-five minutes to half-carry, half-drag Thomas Butler's big listless body up the embankment and back to the fire, where he settled him next to Alexander and Jimmy Butler. He then returned again to the beach below.

In the space of that time, Robert Ivany had assisted four other men up the face of the cliff. When he went down for the fifth time, he saw Henry George Batson's boat finally touch the shore. It brought with it, besides Batson, the semi-conscious fifty-nine-year-old Silas White and the frozen body of Batson's nephew, Martin, aged twenty-six, who had also perished on the way in.

During the next hour or so many more boats and men made their way in through the turbulent waters to Hay Cove. John Butler, Robert Penny, and Robert Ivany worked feverishly to rescue them and bring them up one by one to safety and the warmth of the fire. By now the pain in Butler's injured hand was almost unbearable. Then, as their strength began to wane with the effort of continually scaling the cliffs, a fourth man, Stephen Day from Robinhood, arrived on the scene. Day had also come out to English Harbour earlier in the day for Joseph Penny's funeral. For John Butler and his two companions, Day's appearance was a godsend. He was a big man, exceptionally strong and fit, and he made the monumental task of Butler, Penny, and Ivany much easier. He moved tirelessly up and down the cliff, bringing man after man to the safety and comfort of the fire. He had given most of his own warm outer clothing to the men he was trying to help, yet seemed impervious to the wind and snow that continually blasted his own massive frame. When most of the remaining men had been brought up, Day went back to English Harbour, running most of the way, to get more men to come out and help them bring the survivors back.

Jimmy Butler, still unconscious, was taken to the home of William Ivany on English Head, the closest house, about two miles away. There he was finally coaxed back to life by Ivany's wife. His hands and feet were badly frostbitten, but otherwise he was unharmed. Alexander, his father, had his hands and feet badly frostbitten too. Mrs. Ivany, having treated their frostbitten extremities as best she could, plied them with cup after cup of hot broth and tea, and insisted that they stay there for the night. It was her judicious treatment of their severe frostbite that saved both Alexander's and Jimmy's hands and feet from permanent damage and possible amputation, for which the two would be forever grateful.

By seven o'clock that night the last of the men who had survived the harrowing ordeal had been brought back to English Harbour. The majority of them spent the rest of the night in homes throughout the settlement where they were cared for and had their frostbite and other afflictions attended to by the sympathetic and caring residents. Some, though, were taken by horse and dray or dog teams to their homes in nearby Salmon Cove, Robinhood, and Ship Cove, where their worried families were anxiously awaiting their return. A few of them had by then even recovered enough to leave on their own and make their way back home on foot.

Also brought back to English Harbour were the bodies of the six men who had died; Bob and Charlie Bannister, William Stockley, Martin Batson, James Penny, and Isaac Butler. But for the efforts of John Butler, Robert Penny, Robert Ivany, and Stephen Day, many of the other forty-odd men who landed at the Horse Chops and survived that fateful day would undoubtedly have perished as well.

John Butler would reflect afterwards that it was Joseph Penny's burial that had placed him in English Harbour at that particular time. The significance of this coincidental occurrence was not lost on him. From that day on, whenever he thought about his brother-in-law's funeral, he would be reminded of the terrible sequence of events which had occurred that day, and realize that Penny's death had indirectly contributed to the rescue of many other men from his community.

X
Landfall on Ireland's Eye

At five-thirty-five p.m. on Saturday, eighteen miles south of the Horse Chops, in the darkening kitchen of her house in Old Tilt[10] on Ireland's Eye, Patience Ivany was getting the oil lamp ready for the night when she was startled by loud thumping on her back porch door. With the just lit lamp still in her hands, she quickly went out to see who was there. Before she could open it herself, the door flew open and a wild-looking man burst in and pitched headlong on the floor at her feet. Her loud scream brought her husband, John, and her seventeen-year-old son, William, running from the wood-house where they had been cleaving junks and making splits for the morning fire.

"Who is it, John?" Patience, who was now over her initial shock, asked him, "Do you know him, the poor man?" Already her fright had turned to compassion and concern for the man that now lay snow-and-ice encrusted on her porch floor. In spite of her curiosity, it really didn't matter to her who he was or where he had come from. All that mattered at that moment was that the poor man, whoever he was, was in dire need of help and assistance, and she was willing to do anything within her power to help him.

John wasn't quite sure of the man's identity, but offered a tentative reply. "I think it's Bill Day from Salmon Cove," he told her. Then, upon further examination, believing more firmly that to be the case, he added, "Yes, I'm pretty certain that's who it is. But where in the world

[10] Old Tilt was renamed Ivanhoe in 1917.

did he come from?"

Even in his distorted state, Bill Day's massive bulk was unmistakable. He had been a frequent visitor to Ireland's Eye and had been in John Ivany's house in Old Tilt on many prior occasions.

"He looks like he's almost frozen to death," Patience continued. "How in God's name did he get here? We got to get him into the kitchen, John, and try to get him warmed up. But how will we ever be able to move him, he's so big?"

Day, still on the floor, chose that moment to stir and make his first comment. "John," he croaked, "there's two punt-loads of men out on the Thoroughfare Point. There were two of them already dead when I left. Perhaps the others are too by this time. You'll have to go out and get them." Then, miraculously, he somehow managed to pull himself to his feet and walked unaided into the kitchen and sat down on the daybed.

Ivany urgently told his wife, "You look after him, Patience, and I'll get ready to go out to the point and see what he's talking about." Then he scrambled to pull on his cap and overcoat and ready himself for the trek out to the area where Day said the punts had come ashore. He instructed his son, "Get your stuff on, too, Will, and go next door and get Ned to come with us." Ned Ivany, his first cousin, lived in the closest house to his own. Before leaving, Ivany had also asked Patience to sound the alarm and to get some men together to launch a couple of boats and come around to the point to help them. Minutes later, the three were on their way to the aid of the stricken men.

John, Will, and Ned Ivany did not know what to expect when they got out to the point and feared the worst. Even for them, as familiar as they were with the area, the mile-long slog over the hills, rocks, and uneven tree-covered ground out to the point would be a grueling affair. Yet within the space of twenty minutes they were there. As they neared the spot where Bill Day had told them they would find the stranded men, they could see glimpses of a fire burning in the distance. Encouraged because the presence of a fire surely meant that someone, at least, was still alive, they redoubled their efforts to get there. When they finally arrived on the scene, the Ivanys could see in the eerie light cast by the flickering flames, two men sitting as close as possible to the fire trying to absorb its warmth. Two other men lay on the ground so near the fire that the flames nipped at their clothing and flankers landed on their curled-up bodies where they lay.

"Hallooo the fire! We're coming in," John Ivany shouted to announce his arrival and to make himself heard over the howling wind, "Who are you? Where are you from?"

"Thank God you're here," came the feeble reply. "It's me, John Hiscock from Salmon Cove and that's George Ivany." John Ivany knew both men well but hadn't been able to recognize either of them.

"And that's Joe Goldsworthy and Art White there on the ground," Hiscock added. "There's not much life in them but I think they're still alive. There's two others dead in the punt."

Ivany knew that they had to get these four men back to Old Tilt before they perished out there on the point. He, Will, and Ned could come back afterwards for the dead bodies of the other two men if need be. Yet it was obvious that, with the possible exception of Hiscock, none of them were in any condition to attempt the long and difficult walk back. So immediately John and his companions gathered boughs and brush to increase the intensity of the fire and also to cover the men and keep them warm. Then when help arrived, they would hopefully be in a little better condition to be moved.

"There's boats on the way," Ivany reassured the frozen men. "They'll be here before too long. You just rest and stay warm, and we'll get you back to the house as soon as we can."

For the next twenty minutes, John Ivany and his companions did what they could to keep the four survivors alive. They kept up a continuous conversation with Hiscock to keep him from falling asleep or slipping off into unconsciousness, but the semi-conscious George Ivany and the unconscious Joe Goldsworthy and Art White were still incapable of communication of any kind.

John Ivany was the first one to spot the boats arriving. "There they are, b'ys," he called out, "You'll be alright now. We'll have you home before you know it." There were three large punts, powered by six strong men. The rescuers had brought with them blankets, brin bags, pieces of canvas, coats, caps, and woolen cuffs, as well as flasks of scalding hot tea and brandy. John Hiscock and George Ivany were wrapped up in the blankets to protect them from the cold and placed in the first punt, while Goldsworthy and White, similarly protected, were lowered into the second. The bodies of Charles Day and Edward Pottle, still frozen together, were placed in the third punt, and the three boats left Thoroughfare Point to return to the settlement with their cargoes of frozen men. John, Will, and Ned Ivany made their way back to Old Tilt by land the same way they had come out.

Once they were all back, Patience Ivany and two other women of the community, Mary and Minnie Toope, took charge of the situation. Patience had room enough in her house to accommodate Bill Day and one other man. She chose John Hiscock (perhaps because besides Day, he was still the only coherent one of the lot and she wanted to hear the full story from his own lips), while it was decided that George Ivany would be placed into the overnight care of Ned Ivany and his wife, Joanna. Joe Goldsworthy and Art White, both of whom by now were starting to come around a bit, were entrusted into the care of Mary and Minnie Toope. Pots of hot soup and kettles of steaming tea materialized from nearby houses as other men and women of the community, who by now were fully aware of what was taking place, came bearing woolen blankets, extra warm clothing, and other items meant for the survivors' comforts, and to see them firsthand and find out exactly what had happened.

Patience refused to listen to her husband's suggestions that they place the bodies of Charles Day and Edward Pottle in his store[11] for the night, and insisted instead that they be placed in the seldom-used "parlor room" of the house of her daughter, Priscilla, who lived near-by.

"But they're frozen together, maid. They won't fit on a bed or a couch like that," he argued.

"I know that, John," she explained to her husband, "you'll just have to break them apart. They won't know the difference. But if I went to bed knowing that them poor men were out in the store like that, I wouldn't be able to close my eyes for a minute this night."

Without further argument, John Ivany did as he was told, and he and a few other men undertook the gruesome task of separating the two frozen bodies.

When the survivors were settled away as best they could be for the night, Bill Day, who amazingly was still awake, began to tell them his story. Between gulps of brandy-laced tea, he related how he and the others had been caught unawares by the storm while out on the

[11] Outbuilding or shed.

ice-field just off the Horse Chops, and how they had tried in vain to battle their way to the Horse Chops before having to give up and let themselves be carried up the bay by the wind. He described their harrowing ordeal, and how, when the punt in which George Ivany and Edward Pottle were travelling threatened to capsize, the two men had to be taken onboard with himself and Charles Day. Tears streamed down Patience Ivany's face as she listened to him tell how Charles Day and Edward Pottle had perished along the way. He told them how he himself was on the verge of giving up when they spotted Bonaventure Head, and then realized that they still might have a chance of surviving after all.

"How they must have suffered," Patience thought to herself, "and all just for trying to get a few seals to feed their poor families."

Day continued his story, as if compelled to get it all out before allowing himself to go to sleep. "And then when we got close to Ireland's Eye Harbour, we came across another punt to the leeward of us making for the same place, and we tried to come in together. We were unable to row into Ireland's Eye Harbour because of the wind and had to land out there on the point."

He explained how he had been unable to recognize the man rowing in the other boat as John Hiscock and how Hiscock hadn't been able to recognize him either. Even though they were both from the same community and had grown up together, their features had been so distorted by ice and snow that they hadn't known each other.

"We got the men that were still alive out of the punts and onto the land," he continued, "John had some dry matches and he was able to get a fire started. We left the bodies of the two dead men bide in my punt where they were. Then I left to come here to get help."

He described his arduous journey in from the point. "I knew where I was as soon as I landed, and I knew your house was the closest one. I found it hard going making my way here. Sometimes I'd be so exhausted that I wouldn't be able to take another step, and I'd have to stop and rest for a while. I could hardly see where I was going most of the time either, the snow was that thick. I had to go up over hills and around rocks and through the woods, and to tell you the truth, sometimes I didn't know if I was even going in the right direction. I fell down a lot, and a couple of times I caught myself dozing off. But I'd get revived again somehow and get up and try to go on. I don't know how long it took me to get here, but it was some relief when I got to your house and banged on the door."

In all, Bill Day's trek in from the point had taken him almost an hour, an amazing feat of strength and endurance in his extremely weakened and exhausted condition.

John Hiscock had immediately fallen asleep after being placed in one of the Ivany's upstairs bedrooms and was thus unable to relate his own story to them that night. He would do so the next morning and tell how he, Goldsworthy and White, like Bill Day and the others, had been forced up the bay because they couldn't make land anywhere else. After several hours of constant exposure to the storm, the other two men with him had given up and laid down in the bottom of the punt while he alone continued to row on. And, like Day, he too had all but given up hope when he spotted Bonaventure Head through the snow squalls. Then when he met up with Bill Day in the other boat a short while later, his spirits were lifted further still as they made for the sanctuary of Ireland's Eye together.

St. Nicholas' Church (above) in Salmon Cove and Christ Church in Robinhood/Ship Cove (below) were the scenes of several of the funerals for the victims. (St. Silas's Church in English Harbour, where the funeral services for the victims of that community were conducted, was destroyed by fire shortly after the disaster).

English Harbour (above), with nine deaths, was the hardest hit community, followed by Salmon Cove, now Champneys, (below) with six.

Ice in Trinity Bay (above).
Trouty (below), the scene of Johnny Miller's miraculous escape.

English Head (above).
A sailing and rowing fishing punt (below) similar to those used at the time of the disaster, (PANL A 12-58).

Sealers working on loose ice (above), (PANL A 8-132).
Schooner similar to Capt. Richard Fowlow's Rosscleer (below), (PANL B 4-150).

XI
Searching the Bay

Sunday, February 28th, dawned overcast and cold. Overnight the gale-force winds of the previous day had abated to a stiff twenty-five knot breeze. The heavy snowfall had also ended, and the waters of Trinity Bay, while still rough, had subsided considerably. During the night the ice-field had drifted south and much closer to the land. It now stretched from the Horse Chops to the settlement of Old Perlican on the far south shore, virtually sealing off the entire entrance of the bay, rendering passage in and out of Trinity Bay impossible.

Today, Sunday, would be a day of deep despair and grief for many families in the settlements of Ship Cove, Robinhood, Salmon Cove, English Harbour, Trinity, Trinity South, and Green Bay. Sadly, a number of the men from these communities who had been caught out on the ice-field in Saturday's storm were already confirmed dead. Their bodies had been recovered and given into the keeping of their families for burial. In these communities, and indeed in many others all over the bay, dozens of other men were still missing while their families and relatives could only hope and pray that they had been able to take refuge somewhere from the storm and would soon be making their way home to them again.

As the morning progressed and the news of the deaths and the large number of men still missing spread from community to community, the magnitude of the disaster of the previous day slowly began to sink in. At the start of the Sunday morning, the known death toll stood at eight with more than sixty men still unaccounted for. As small groups of men slowly made their way back home during the day, some by punt and some on foot from the places where they had landed and taken shelter, the number of missing men was gradually reduced until by nightfall it was down to thirty or less. By then, though, the death toll had risen to ten with the recovery of two more bodies from a swamped punt found out in the bay.

At eight-thirty that morning, Captain Richard Fowlow had answered a knock on his door in Pease Cove (Trinity East) to find two men wishing to talk to him. They were Elias and Norman Penny, from English Harbour, and Fowlow could tell by their faces that they were very concerned about something.

"Captain Fowlow, sir," Elias Penny started, "two of our brothers never came home last night, and we fear they might be lost. Some of us went out in our punts to look for them early this morning but it's still pretty rough out there and we couldn't do much with it. We'd never be able to cover much of the bay in the punts anyway, it would take us days."

"What we came to ask you, Captain," interjected Norman Penny, "is whether you'd consider taking us out in your schooner? We know it's a lot to ask, but we can't think of anything else."

The early morning visit of Elias and Norman Penny prompted Richard Fowlow to finally make the decision that he himself had already been contemplating since getting out of bed two hours earlier. The *Rosscleer*, having been fitted out a few days previously for the off-shore seal fishery, was in a state of readiness and just waiting for favourable weather and ice conditions before heading for the Front. It would only take an hour or so to get her underway.

"Yes, b'ys," he told them, "I'll take you out. But we'll have to get a few more men to go with us. I'll round up some of my regular hands and maybe a few more. Let's run up our flag, and then we'll go and have a look."

At ten. a.m. the *Rosscleer* swung out past Skerwink Rock making for the Horse Chops with a volunteer crew of fourteen men on board. Equipped with spy glasses, a half dozen men had taken up positions in the rigging to scan the ice and the water for signs of survivors or abandoned punts. From the Horse Chops, Fowlow sailed the *Rosscleer* along the edge of the ice-field, which by that time was only two miles off from English Head, all the way across Trinity Bay to Old Perlican, a distance of some twenty miles. Although they stopped to investigate a few possible sightings that later proved fruitless upon closer examination, their slow methodical search of the ice-field from the vantage point of the schooner failed to turn up anything of note. When they reached Old Perlican, Fowlow consulted with his crew.

"What do you think we should do now, b'ys?" he asked them. "Will we turn around and go back? Or should we continue on down as far as Hant's Harbour and have a look around in that area? If any of them were forced to go with the wind yesterday or last night, that's where they might have ended up with that northeast wind."

"Continue on, Captain," came the loud chorus of replies.

"Are all hands game for that? We'll probably be gone all night, maybe longer," Fowlow followed up. He wanted to be certain that all hands on board were in agreement. Again came the chorus, "Yes, sir," and Fowlow, with the unanimous agreement of his volunteer crew, now steered the *Rosscleer* for Hant's Harbour, running a zig-zag course parallel to the shore to keep a look-out for survivors.

An hour into their new course, one of the men in the rigging called down, "There's something off to the starboard, Captain Fowlow. Looks like it might be a swamped punt."

A few minutes later they closed in on a semi-submerged punt. An oar and a piggin floated in the water close by. The water-filled punt, however, was otherwise empty and there was no further evidence of any kind in the vicinity to give the men on the schooner any hope or encouragement of finding anything else of relevance. After searching the immediate area for another half hour or so, they left to resume their search farther south.

At three p.m. they passed Hant's Harbour and were a little ways off Scilly Cove,[12] when the cry came down from aloft that another punt had been sighted. This time when they rounded up to the stranded punt, which, like the first one was also filled with water, they discovered that it contained the bodies of two men.

"Anyone know who they are?" queried Fowlow from his position at the helm.

"Tis Solomon Penny and John Nurse," someone responded, "from Green Bay."[13]

The bodies of the two drowned men were under the tawts of the punt when they were found. It was obvious that they had rowed as long as they could, and when they had become too exhausted to continue any farther, had given up and laid down in the bottom of the punt. After they were taken on board and placed in the hold of the

---

[12] Scilly Cove was renamed Winterton in 1912 in honour of former Prime Minister Sir James S. Winter.

[13] A tiny fishing settlement, now deserted, about three miles northeast of English Head.

Rosscleer, Fowlow and his crew continued to scour the immediate area for another hour. Their further efforts proved fruitless, and Captain Fowlow decided to move on again. He wanted to put a man ashore at Heart's Content to send a telegraph to Trinity to inform the railroad operator there of the recovery of Solomon Penny and John Nurse's bodies.

With that done and some daylight still left, Fowlow and his crew decided to plod on a little farther into the bottom of the bay, perhaps as far as Heart's Delight, where they would probably spend the night. Ice on the south shore of the bay, however, prevented the *Rosscleer* from landing there and Fowlow decided that their best bet was to cut across the bay to spend the night in the shelter of Deer Harbour. Both he and his crew were somewhat reluctant to leave the south shore, though, because shortly after arriving off Heart's Delight, they had spotted smoke rising from an isolated stretch of woods on the shore. They believed it had been a signal meant for them, but the ice had prevented them from exploring its origin before leaving.

At first light Monday morning, they backtracked to resume their search on the south side of the bay. The wind was still blowing fairly hard from the northeast and overnight the temperature had fallen several more degrees. The bay was now caught over. It was inches thick in places, which hindered the schooner somewhat in its forward progress. The ice on the south shore of the bay in the vicinity of Heart's Delight and the other settlements farther south was still tightly packed, again making it impossible for Fowlow to bring the schooner in as close to the shore as he had hoped to. Their only alternative now was to range up and down the edge of the ice and maintain their vigil from a distance.

Late in the morning the men in the rigging spotted

what they thought were two more punts on the ice between themselves and the shore. Fowlow sailed the *Rosscleer* in as close as he dared, and then dispatched four men in a punt to go to them. "Let's pray there's men in them alive," he told them. "Take some blankets and a bit of grub and water with you, b'ys, just in case. God speed, and get back as soon as you can."

To his great disappointment and dismay, however, the four men returned an hour later only to report that the two punts had been empty when they reached them.

"Maybe that was the smoke we saw last evening," one of the crew suggested. "Perhaps they made their way to shore on the ice and were trying to signal us."

"I hope to God you're right," replied Fowlow, "at least if they're on the land they'll be alright. They'll manage to get home somehow."

Later in the afternoon they spied yet another punt, this time out in the open water. As they approached it, to their astonishment, three more punts hove into view not far away. This time, even from that distance, Fowlow and the others could see men rowing these punts, a clear indication that at least some of the men in them were still alive. When the punts, breaking through the skim of ice, finally came alongside, the captain and crew of the *Rosscleer* found, to their great delight, that the sixteen men in them, all from the Trinity Bight area, were alive and well. Having been blown up the bay on Saturday evening, the men had spent the night on the ice near Heart's Delight. They had been spotted and rescued by the people of the area on Sunday morning and were now making their way back home.

After hearing their story, Fowlow asked them, "Were you planning to row all the way back? If you are, why not come on board with us. But we'll have to finish our search of the bay first." After a brief discussion among themselves, the sixteen men agreed to take Fowlow up on his offer of passage home on his schooner, and they and their punts were hoisted up onto the deck of the ***Rosscleer***.

Again, as on Sunday, the schooner was unable to land on the south side of the bay because of the thick ice close to shore, and after searching without further success until darkness set in on Monday evening, Captain Fowlow decided to call it quits and set his course for Trinity. He and his crew arrived there about nine o'clock Tuesday morning. Their progress had been impeded by newly formed ice that prevented them from making better time. In their two full days of searching, they had found one swamped punt containing two dead bodies, three more abandoned water-filled punts and some floating debris – and sixteen safe and happy men making their way back home to their waiting families.

XII
Trinity Bight Buries Its Dead

During the two days that Captain Richard Fowlow and his fourteen-man volunteer crew had spent searching the ice-field and the south shore of Trinity Bay in the *Rosscleer*, an armada of punts had been scouring the north shore of the bay, from Bonaventure Head to the Horse Chops, looking for survivors. When the weather and water conditions finally permitted, they poked into every small cove and indentation of the shoreline looking for stranded men, abandoned punts, or any other sign that someone may have been there. Their combined efforts brought back more than two dozen men from places all over the north shore where they had been forced to land and take shelter from the storm. Having been driven ashore and forced to spend Saturday night wherever they were able to land, and in some cases part or all of Sunday as well, they were all in poor condition. Owing their lives to the unstinting efforts of the multitude of men who had gone out to search for them, the rescued seal hunters all arrived back home severely frostbitten, cold, hungry, and bone weary but alive. Some of them had also received various other injuries in their ordeal.

The searchers also brought back with them the bodies of two more victims of Saturday's terrible storm. They were twenty-year-old Tobias Penny, of English Harbour, and John Penny, aged forty, from Salmon Cove. Both bodies had been found and recovered in the vicinity of the Horse Chops. Tobias Penny's body had been discovered in a gulch about halfway between Hay Cove and Green Bay where his water-filled punt was found wallowing in the water only a few feet from shore. The men who found him were of the opinion that he had perished just before reaching the land and that his unmanned punt had eventually taken him to that secluded gulch. There was no sign of Reuben Pottle, who was known to have left the ice-field in the punt with him. The body of John Penny was found on the beach in a partially obscured indentation on English Head, about two and a half miles farther south. It appeared obvious that he had been able to make it to shore alive but had expired sometime after arriving there. His punt was nowhere to be found.

Late Sunday afternoon, word was received in English Harbour that the body of another of its residents, William Barnes, had been recovered on Ireland's Eye, where he and a number of other men had come ashore. The fifty-year-old Barnes had perished before reaching land.

By end of day on Monday, February 29th (1892 being a leap year), the official death count stood at thirteen, and eleven other men were still missing and now presumed dead. The trickle of men returning from whence they had been stranded or taken shelter from the storm had finally stopped, and although searchers still scoured the bay for the eleven missing men, hope for their safe return had all but been abandoned.

On Tuesday, March 1st, the communities of the Parish of Trinity East[14] began to bury their dead. English Harbour was the hardest hit, with five confirmed deaths and four men missing and presumed dead. Salmon Cove followed with a total of six, Ship Cove/Robinhood with four, and

---

[14] The Parish of Trinity East at the time encompassed the communities of Trinity East, Ship Cove, Robinhood, Lockston, English Harbour and Green Bay.

Green Bay with two. Trinity South, in the Parish of Trinity (Proper) also listed three men as missing and presumed dead. The final casualty count stood at twenty-four.

The first funerals to be conducted were those of Bob and Charlie Bannister. People from Ship Cove and Robinhood, as well as many others from the neighboring settlements, crammed every available inch of space in Christ Church at ten o'clock Tuesday morning for the joint burial service of Bannister and his son. Many men and women who arrived too late to get a place inside the church filled the outer vestibule while still others waited outside on the church steps or in the churchyard while the funeral service was being conducted inside by the Rev. John Godden. Godden was the Church of England Minister for the Parish of Trinity East at the time. There was hardly a dry eye in the congregation. It was one of the saddest funerals ever held in the area. Grown men, inured by years of hardship and deprivation, wept openly like small children knowing that these were just the first of many funerals to be held in the coming days. Clara Ballett sat between her parents in the center of the church, wringing her hands and sobbing softly. Her dream of one day having Charlie Bannister for her husband was dashed forever.

The graves for Bob and Charlie Bannister had been dug with great difficulty the previous day. A contingent of men had taken turns with their pick-axes, shovels, and crowbars to open up the hard frozen ground. Every half hour or so they would have to light a fire to heat the ground up enough to enable them to dig down a few more inches. It took the combined efforts of a half dozen strong, sweating able-bodied men to get the job completed in time for the burials.

Flora Bannister, bereaved widow and mother, was a strong woman. Her faith had seen her through many difficult times in her life. During the three days in which her husband and her youngest son were waking in the front room of her house, she had hovered over the endless succession of relatives and visitors who had come to participate in the wake, ensuring that they all had a cup of tea and something to eat before they left. She had shown them all "poor old Bob's" and "poor little Charlie's" frozen hands, always placing her own hand somewhere on their corpses as if trying to draw comfort from their cold bodies. After her initial shock, she had cried very little. In the ensuing three days, she hadn't slept much and had managed to get through the waking period and the funeral service in the church without much outward display of emotion. Her stoicism ended, though, when they were lowering the coffins of her two lost loved ones into their graves and the finality of Bob's and Charlie's deaths fully hit her. Then she broke down and wept uncontrollably.

Flora's only consolation was that her two remaining sons, John and Job, who had themselves been caught out in the storm, had made their way safely back to shore. Now they, along with her five daughters and her many in-laws, comforted her as best they could – but she was inconsolable. When they finally took her home, she refused to enter her house. "I'll never be able to set foot in there again," she moaned, "I can't live there anymore without Bob and Charlie. I just couldn't do it."

"You won't have to, Mother," her oldest son, John, told her and gently led her away, "You can come and live with me and Alice for as long as you want to." Shortly afterward she had John and Job retrieve her clothes and a few of her most precious possessions from the house and then board up its windows and doors. True to her word, she would never return there again.

Immediately following the burial of Bob and Charlie Bannister, the Rev. Godden left to go to St. Nicholas' Church in Salmon Cove to conduct the one p.m. funeral service of John Penny, and from there on to St. Silas's Church in English Harbour for the four o'clock funeral services of Tobias Penny and Martin Batson.

On Wednesday, the funerals continued with Godden performing burial services for William Stockley and Isaac Butler of Robinhood, and Charles Day of Salmon Cove. Among the men and women who crowded St. Nicholas' Church in Salmon Cove for Day's funeral was Emma Bailey of Cuckhold's Cove, Charles' betrothed. The twenty-year old woman, as reserved and withdrawn as Charles himself, was too shy and timid to come forward to sit up in front with Charles' family. She sat in the back of the church for the duration of the service where she wept quietly. She would never get over her devastation at Charles' death or marry in her lifetime. She lived out her days as a spinster in the family house in Cuckhold's Cove which she eventually inherited from her parents upon their deaths.

And finally on Thursday, March 3rd, the Rev. Godden buried the last of the men from his parish who had perished in the storm, Solomon Penny and John Nurse of Green Bay. The weary minister was himself moved and shaken by the events of the previous few days. Never before had he held so many funeral services in such a short space of time, and the significance of the loss of so many men from his parish was wearing on him badly. Late that evening he retired to the vestry of Christ Church in Robinhood/Ship Cove (which at the time served as the central church for the Parish of Trinity East) to update the Parish Death Register. In the dim light of the oil lamp and in his small neat handwriting, he entered the names of the ten men whom he had just buried:

Robert Bannister, Ship Cove, age 62
Charles Bannister, Ship Cove, age 18
John Penny, Salmon Cove, age 40
Tobias Penny, English Harbour, age 20
Martin Batson, English Harbour, age 28
Bill Stockley, Robinhood, age 62
Isaac Butler, Robinhood, age 18
Charles Day, Salmon Cove, age 20
Solomon Penny, Green Bay, age 22
John Nurse, Green Bay, age 32

In the column headed Cause of Death, he carefully penned the words "Cold & Exhaustion" beside each name. The funeral services for the other three men whose bodies had been recovered, William Barnes, Edward Pottle, and James Penny, were conducted in the Methodist Church in English Harbour.

Ten days later, after a due period of waiting, Reverend Godden took out the Death Register once again to record the names of those still missing and presumed dead. One by one, he entered the names of:

George Moore, Trinity South, age 42
John Moore, Trinity South, age 32
Jacob Moore, Trinity South, age 26
John Batson, English Harbour
William Batson, English Harbour
Arthur Batson, English Harbour
Reuben Pottle, English Harbour
Charles Nurse, Salmon Cove, age 25
William Nurse, Salmon Cove, age 20
Henry Nurse, Salmon Cove, age 27
George Nurse, Salmon Cove, age 42

This time, in the Cause of Death column he carefully wrote beside the name of George Moore, the first one entered, the words, "Perished in the Bay with 10 others who were never heard of." Beside each of the other names that followed, he simply wrote, "Perished in the Bay."

As he scanned the entries he had just made, his eyes focused for several seconds on the names of the four Nurse brothers from Salmon Cove, and he recalled the special service that he had conducted for them a few days earlier. When the first round of burials had been completed, he had been approached by the three bereaved Nurse widows beseeching him to do something for their lost husbands too. Mary Anne, the widow of George Nurse and the spokesperson for the group, told him, "Reverend Godden, I know we'll never be able to bury the bodies of our husbands in the graveyard like the others, but we'd rest a lot easier if we knew that they at least had a proper church service to see them off." Then she asked him to hold what she referred to as a "special memorial service for George, Charlie, Henry, and young Billy."

Two days later, acceding to their request, he conducted the memorial service that the grieving women had requested. For one last time the people of the area packed St. Nicholas' Church in Salmon Cove. Most were already seated in their places when the three Nurse widows arrived and made their way up to the front of the church. Their children and many of their closest relatives trailed behind them. Mary Anne led the feeble William Nurse, her father-in-law and the father of the four drowned brothers, to his pew, and settled him down between herself and her other two sisters-in-law.

As he waited for the service to begin, William Nurse listened to the poignant organ strains of *Eternal Father,*

Strong to Save, which sounded vaguely familiar and comforting to him, while his eyes strayed over the crowded church. He wondered what everyone was doing there, why he himself was there, and why Mary Anne was crying and holding his hand so tightly. Then his mind cleared momentarily and the searing, excruciating reality that he had lost his four sons – all of them – flooded his mind with brutal clarity and destroyed what was left of it. He slipped back into his own, isolated, comfortable world for the last time, and would never again emerge from it in the four remaining years of his existence.

XIII
Survival

The grief-stricken communities of Trinity Bight reeled from their staggering loss. Thirteen of their number had been laid to rest, but the residents were still haunted and tormented by the knowledge that the bodies of eleven others were still somewhere out in the depths of the bay. In almost every community in the Bight, oil lamps burned late into the night as relatives and friends congregated in the houses of the grieving families to provide company and to give whatever comfort and solace they could to the bereaved.

A pall of gloom and despair had settled over the area. The horrific disaster of February 27th continued to dominate the thoughts and conversation of men, women, and children everywhere as they tried to get on with their daily lives. The men and boys who had been caught out in the storm had all suffered some degree of frostbite, especially to their hands, feet, and other extremities. Most, though, had avoided serious permanent damage by employing the age-old remedy of rubbing snow into their frozen flesh to facilitate the thawing out process, or had their frostbite and other injuries effectively treated by family members upon returning home.

One of the busiest men in the bay in the days and weeks following the tragic deaths of the twenty-four men was Dr. White of Trinity, whose area of responsibility included all of the communities on the north shore of Trinity Bay from Bonaventure Head to Green Bay. Many men and boys whose frostbite was still serious despite the treatment they had already received before coming to see him, patiently waited their turn in his clinic to have their damaged flesh and injured bodies seen to. Amputations of fingers and toes that were too far gone to be saved were the order of the day, and in some of the more extreme cases, men had to have their feet amputated before the spreading gangrene took their legs, and perhaps their lives as well. Hardly a man who had been caught out in the storm escaped unscathed. Most of them would take shriveled or darkened patches of skin and other scars of that day, both physical and psychological, to their graves.

Amid all the sadness and sorrow, however, there was great rejoicing and thanksgiving for the approximately one hundred and seventy-five men whose lives had been spared. For every death, there were a dozen stories of survival and salvation, some so astonishing and miraculous as to defy belief.

Perhaps the most amazing story of all was that of fifteen-year-old Johnny Miller of Trouty. On Friday night, the eve of the storm, he had been staying overnight with his grandparents in English Harbour, and when he got up on Saturday morning and saw all the other men and boys of the settlement leaving to row out to the ice-field, he was determined that he would do likewise. Without his grandfather's knowledge or consent, the impulsive boy took the old man's small punt and, with only himself to do the rowing, followed the others out into the bay. When the storm broke he, like everybody else, scrambled to leave the ice-field and tried to make his way back to shore. As did most of the other men who had been in the same area with him at the time, he too headed for the Horse Chops. His fifteen-year-old body, however, did not have the strength or the stamina to make any significant headway against the wind, and unable to effectively propel the punt along, he was gradually pushed farther south and out into the open bay as he tried in vain to row to shore. Although he was in great peril, his main concern at the moment was what punishment he would receive from his grandfather on returning home for taking the punt out without his permission.

A half hour after leaving the ice-field, Johnny Miller's fortunes took a serious turn for the worse when one of his oars snapped. And then, a short time later, the other one which he had been trying to use as a sculling oar to steer the punt along, was wrenched from his hands by a crashing wave. Without a jib sail or any other means of propulsion, he had no way of getting himself to shore. In great despair because he now finally recognized the extreme seriousness of his situation, he held on to the tawt as the little punt pitched and bucked in the gale-force wind and churning sea while the freezing spray continued to coat both the punt and himself. After a while he simply gave up and, resigned to his fate, laid down in the punt and eventually drifted off to sleep.

At six o'clock that evening, almost seven hours later, Arthur Miller, Johnny's uncle, was securing his own boat to the wharf of his fishing stage in Trouty, about eight miles south of English Harbour, when in the gathering darkness he caught a fleeting glimpse of what he thought was a punt bobbing around in the narrow channel that led into the sheltered cove of Trouty itself. Curious, he untied his punt again and rowed out to investigate, and when he did he discovered to his utter disbelief his nephew curled up in the bottom of the drifting punt. He brought the ice-covered unconscious boy in and carried him to his own house, it being the closest one, and sent one of his daughters to fetch the boy's parents who lived nearby. They all worked feverishly to try to revive him and bring him back to life. Miraculously, by eight o'clock that same evening, Johnny Miller was sitting up at the kitchen table of his uncle's house drinking soup and tea and telling his incredible story. Although still frightened by his harrowing experience and narrow escape, he was otherwise unharmed.

The people of Trouty would accept no other explanation but that the hand of God Himself had delivered the boy, against all possible odds, right to his own doorstep in the storm, unharmed despite the severity of the storm, the freezing temperature, and the icy spray that coated him from head to foot. They calculated, too, that the winds and the tides on Saturday afternoon by rights should have carried him and the powerless punt in which he was travelling much farther south toward the other side of the bay, or perhaps even out into the open ocean. Having escaped this first impulsive attempt to get a seal or two, Johnny Miller would go on to live to be a spry old man of eighty and be able to tell his many grand-children and great-grand-children about his wonderful adventure that day.

Another miraculous escape occurred just a few miles farther south on the same stretch of coastline. It was well after dark when Heber Barnes and his fourteen-year-old son, Eli, clawed their way ashore onto the steep cliffs between Trouty and Bonaventure Head. Their punt was on the verge of sinking when they neared land and they had barely been able to make it ashore before it went under. They were not sure where they had landed, and, in the darkness, were only able to make their way a few feet up onto the steep slippery rocks. There, clinging to a small ledge on the face of the cliff with the waves and freezing spray at their feet, they spent the night.

Heber Barnes tried to drape his big body over his son's smaller frame to shelter him from the brunt of the storm. He reassured the boy over and over that everything would be alright in the morning. Fortunately, both he and his son were clad in their warmest winter clothing and were thus able to ward off the worst of the bitter frost. Several times during the night they found themselves slipping down the face of the cliff and had to claw their way back up to their ledge again. Although they both knew that they were in extreme peril and might not live to see the light of day, their indomitable spirits wouldn't permit either of them to give up.

The next morning, after almost ten agonizing, terror-filled hours of great suffering and extreme discomfort, when they could finally see where they were, they managed to inch their way by degrees farther up the cliff until they reached the tree-line. From there they somehow forced their stiff, wet, frozen bodies inland through the woods, climbing ever upward on the steep heavily forested incline, until they eventually came across a well-used slide-path that ran between Old Bonaventure and Trouty. By a stroke of good luck, they were almost immediately spotted by a man named Baxter Hodder who happened to be hauling firewood in the area at the time, and he jettisoned his load of wood to make room on the sled and took Heber Barnes and his son by dog team to his own house in Old Bonaventure. There he and his wife tended to them. Both Heber Barnes and his son Eli were so badly frostbitten that they would afterward have to have some of their fingers and toes amputated, and various other parts of their bodies treated for serious frostbite damage. They had, however, both survived their terrible ordeal and lived to see another day.

An equally dramatic escape involved five men who had left English Harbour for the ice-field on Saturday morning. They were Martin Bugden, William Penny (Senior), William Penny (Junior), Edward Bugden, and Francis Barnes, in two punts of sixteen and fifteen feet length respectively. When they were forced by the storm to leave the ice-field at eleven a.m., they too, like most others, rowed for the Horse Chops. After an hour and a half of hard rowing, they concluded that they would not be able to make it all the way in against the heavy headwind, and therefore changed their minds and set their course for the south side of the bay. Using their small sails to assist them in their rowing, they spent the next four hours clinging to their oars as the turbulent sea pounded them mercilessly and freezing spray coated their bodies. Despite their efforts to keep bearing to the southwest, toward Bonaventure Head and Ireland's Eye, where they had hoped to land, they were being continually driven, without realizing it, almost due south as they moved along in the near-zero visibility.

Eventually the two punts grated upon solid ice, and the men thought that they had somehow been driven back onto the ice-field. Their discouragement at finding themselves practically back where they had started devastated them, and they lost hope. Then, miraculously, through a momentary break in the weather, they spied houses not more than half a mile in the distance.

"That's Daniel's Cove," cried Francis Barnes, "I'm sure of it."

"Thanks be to Jesus, we're saved," one of the others shouted. "But how in God's name did we wind up way over here? I was certain we were heading up the bottom of the bay."

"Never mind that now," someone else chimed in, "We're here, and that's all that matters."

"We'll have to drag the boats the rest of the way," added Barnes, estimating that there was about a half mile of thickly packed ice between themselves and the land. "We can't abandon them because there might be patches of open water between here and the shore, and we'll need them again."

Thirty minutes later the five exhausted, wet, frostbitten, and emotionally spent men, dragging their punts behind them, stepped onto solid land in Daniel's Cove. A number of men from the community had seen them making their way in over the ice and came out to assist them.

Later that night, as they were recovering in the house of Gus Coombs and his wife, Maude, the five men discussed their ordeal. They concluded that if they hadn't come ashore when they did and had to spend the night out in the water in their punts or out on the ice, they would not have survived.

Farther down the bay, seventeen other men, most of them also from the Trinity Bight area, were saved by the keen eyesight of Sadie Crocker. From the kitchen window of her house in Heart's Delight, she had been trying to keep an eye on the conditions out in the bay whenever a lull in the driving snow permitted her to do so. It was a habit that she, a life-long chronic worrier, had long since fallen into when it concerned the safety and welfare of her own family members and others who made their living out on the water.

"I hope there's no poor souls out there today," she thought to herself, "Tis not fit for man nor beast. I don't think I've ever seen it any worse." The thought had scarcely passed through her mind when her sharp eyes detected a number of black dots out on the water.

"My goodness," she exclaimed, "That must be punts." Over the next five minutes, between snow squalls, she tried to count the dots and finally determined that there were five of them. Long accustomed to the ravages of the sea, she immediately assumed that the punts were in trouble and sounded the alarm in the community. A rescue party was organized to go out and bring the men back to shore. When they were finally brought in, the seventeen men were as exhausted, wet, ice-coated, and frostbitten as their counterparts who had landed at Daniel's Cove. They too would have undoubtedly perished in a few more hours if they hadn't been spotted in time by Sadie Crocker's keen eyes and rescued by the good people of Heart's Delight.

Yet another dramatic escape took place in the same general area. Earlier in the day, as the storm was rapidly increasing in intensity, three punt-loads of men who had been situated on the ice mid-way between the Horse Chops and the ice-field's southernmost tip off Old Perlican, made the decision to stay where they were and take their chances on the ice. They were joined by four more punt-loads of men who had been hunting seals nearby. The two groups, when combined, numbered twenty-one in all. The consensus of opinion among them, swayed in no small measure by the influence of a man named Gilbert Peddle, was that the large ice-pan on which they were standing was preferable to trying for shore in the six or seven miles of extremely violent waters that separated them from the nearest land.

By the time the storm reached its height, many of the men had changed their opinions and wished that they had left earlier to try to make it to shore, for the pan of ice that they were standing on had suddenly broken away from the main ice-pack and was set adrift in the bay. But once more they decided to stay on the ice, convinced yet again by the persuasive Peddle that they were still safer there than out on the water. Growing colder, wetter, hungrier, and more discouraged as the hours slowly passed, the men prayed that the storm would soon let up and allow them to make their way home.

In spite of their supplications, the storm continued to worsen and rage around them, and many of them began to lose hope. They turned their punts over on their sides to provide some shelter. At one point late in the night the men were so cold that they decided to burn one of the punts in an attempt to keep some warmth in their freezing bodies. They shared what little food and water they had between them, and kept up a constant stream of conversation with each other to stay awake and as alert as possible, and to give each other reassurance and encouragement. Sometimes they sang songs and hymns or simply prayed. When the first punt burned down, they set fire to a second one to avoid freezing to death there on the ice. Sometimes they danced or walked around to keep their circulation going and at others times just sat or laid on the ice in the lun of the overturned punts, huddled together to conserve their waning strength and energy until the storm ended and they could go home.

The minutes and the hours passed agonizingly slow as they all feared for their lives, but eventually morning broke and the storm abated, and the twenty-one men were able to make their way back to shore in their five remaining punts. Their decision to remain on the ice during the storm had, in retrospect, been a wise one, as not a single life was lost. Afterwards, Gilbert Peddle would say, "If we had gone off in that raging water in them flimsy little punts, I daresay we'd all be dead by now."

Another narrow escape was that of William Ivany, of English Harbour, and his three sons, James, Walter, and Mark. Like many others, they had been unable to land anywhere on the north shore and had been driven up the bay until they were in the general vicinity of Heart's Delight on the south shore. Before they could land, however, the seams of their punt, which had borne them all that distance, parted and it began to fill with water. Almost two miles from shore, they had no choice but to abandon her and get out on a nearby ice-pan where they were forced to spend the night. Without any kind of shelter or the means of making a fire, they barely survived the night. When they were discovered by some men from the area the next morning, they were all in extremely bad shape, especially the youngest son, Mark. He had to be moved from the ice-pan to the rescuers' boat wrapped in a sail. Both of his feet were completely frozen and he was thought to be dying.

All four were taken to Shoal Bay, a tiny fishing settlement above Heart's Delight, where they were treated by the wives of the men who had found them. Besides Mark, the rest of them were also severely frostbitten and in great pain and discomfort. Over the next two days, however, they gradually recovered and shortly afterward were treated by Dr. Anderson who came over from Heart's Content to see them. The doctor had great praise for the manner in which the women had used snow-water from the bay to treat the frostbitten men before he got there. Amazingly, none of them would lose any of their frozen extremities, even Mark, although he would lose some of the flesh of his feet and legs, and suffer recurring discomfort in that area for the rest of his life. Still, William Ivany and his three sons had survived their terrible ordeal, thanks to the men of Shoal Bay and their good wives. A few days later they were able to make their way back home to English Harbour.

Scores of other men and boys somehow managed to make their way to shore after leaving the ice, finding shelter from the storm on the cliffs or in the woods, often in places far removed from their homes. Very few of the two hundred men who had rowed out on Saturday morning had been able to make their way directly back to the communities from which they had come. It took some of them as much as two full days to eventually get back, on foot or by whatever other means were available to them, to the homes from which they had set out that beautiful early Saturday morning.

Many others who had elected to wait out the storm on the ice-field also somehow survived the night and were able to make their way home by punt when the storm abated on Sunday morning. Many of them had burned the oily carcasses of the seals that they had caught to keep themselves warm and fed during the night.

A short while after the disaster, eighty-four-year-old Dora Penny of English Harbour perhaps spoke for all the people of Trinity Bay when she stood up in church and offered her own thoughts on the matter. "We must continue to mourn the loss of our dear departed loved ones, and pray for their souls," she told the congregation, "but we should be louder in our thanks to God for saving all the others. I doubt that ever before did so many miracles happen in one place as happened here in our own bay these past few days. Let God's will be done, for we are all in the hollow of His hand. Amen."

XIV
The Aftermath

Following the disastrous events of February 27th, the widows and the families of the men who had perished in the storm were left in dire circumstances. With their husbands now deceased, the women had virtually no means of supporting themselves and their children. Their husbands' fishing had been their sole source of livelihood. In recognition of their desperate situation, a relief fund for the victims' families was set up in St. John's. Proposed by His Excellency, Governor Whiteway, and initiated by his own substantial personal donation along with a sizeable contribution from the Responsible Government, the establishment of the relief fund and the generous contributions made to it by the citizens of St. John's and other areas of Newfoundland helped to ease the financial burden of the affected families, at least temporarily. The Governor's own brother, Austin R. Whiteway, Esq., a barrister in London, England, sent a donation of five hundred dollars on behalf of himself and a number of his colleagues. Queen Victoria, when informed of the disaster, personally authorized the payment of an additional ten pounds for each affected family to be included in the relief fund. The proceeds from the fund enabled the bereaved families to make it through the coming year and perhaps beyond, and in many ways made the saddened lives of the widows and their sons and daughters a little more bearable. Most of these women, however, would eventually have to depend on other family members or re-marry to ensure their own continued well-being and survival, as well as that of their children.

When the initial shock of the great tragedy had subsided somewhat and the people of Trinity Bay were able to look back upon what had happened on that fateful Saturday with a little more objectivity, they began to ask the inevitable questions. How could so many experienced fishermen, most of them seasoned veterans of the salt water, have misread the weather so badly? If a few, like Eliol Tavener, had anticipated the advancing storm and turned back, why hadn't the others? In their fervor for a few seals, were the rest of them so blind to the obvious indicators of deteriorating weather that they had unwittingly put their lives in such great jeopardy? Or had they seen the signs and simply ignored them and decided to stay there and take their chances?

Some of the survivors would say afterward that if they had been able to relive that day they would have paid more attention to the sudden drop in the temperature and the darkening sky looming in the north-east, and would have done things differently. With the benefit of hindsight, this position was difficult to argue against. Most of the men who had been out on the ice at the time, however, stood firm in their conviction that the storm had advanced upon them too quickly, leaving them with very little time in which to react. They were all united in the opinion, as well, that they had never before seen a storm descend with such sudden savagery, and were simply not prepared for it. Another factor attributing to the severity of the situation was that many of the men, after leaving their punts, had already gone some considerable distance out on the ice-field before the storm broke. Valuable time was lost in making their way back to their boats, thus placing the men at a serious disadvantage right from the start.

The heavy tides that preceded the storm were in retrospect another significant sign of the impending change in the weather that seemed to have been ignored at the time. It made the escape of the men all the more difficult because the ice upon which they were standing began to break up under the enormous strain of the undertow, leaving them vulnerable to being swallowed by the large patches of water that suddenly opened up all around them. In many cases their retreat was barred, making it extremely difficult and dangerous for them to retrace their steps back to their punts.

Perhaps the most burning question of all was why so many of the men had headed for the Horse Chops against the full force of the wind instead of letting it take them farther south in the bay? The obvious answer, that it was the closest point of land, failed to convince many people of the wisdom of this decision. Surely, they argued, with an extremely heavy sea, opting to try to row three or four miles into the teeth of a gale in such tiny boats had been sheer folly in the first place, a flawed decision right from the beginning. As evidence, they would point to the fact that most of the thirteen men whose bodies had been recovered, and perhaps all or most of the other eleven men who were still missing, had died trying to reach the Horse Chops.

Invariably, some of the forty-odd men who had somehow managed to battle their way ashore on or near the Horse Chops would argue that they themselves were living proof that they had done the only reasonable thing in the circumstances. To allow themselves to be carried southward by the wind would have entailed, they claimed, distances of upwards of twenty miles or more, five or six times the distance to the Horse Chops, in waters so turbulent that they feared they would never have made it safely to shore anywhere in the bay.

Still, the reality of the situation was that upwards of a quarter of the men who had attempted to row to the Horse Chops had died in the attempt, a staggering percentage, while the vast majority of men from the Trinity Bight area who had headed elsewhere, perhaps as many as sixty or seventy of them, lived to tell their tales. Among those who had taken the option of heading south or south-west, either immediately upon leaving the ice-field or having done so after being forced to abandon their attempt to row to the Horse Chops, only five of the confirmed dead – Charles Day, Edward Pottle, William Barnes, Solomon Penny, and John Nurse – were known to have perished in the attempt. As well, the large number of men who had gone out to the ice-field from Old Bonaventure, New Bonaventure, Ireland's Eye, and other communities farther south in the bay, had, despite their many harrowing experiences and narrow escapes, all been carried safely home by the wind without any casualties at all.

Thirdly, people asked, could anything else have been done to mitigate the large number of deaths? In particular, this question was directed at the Government in St. John's. The Government of the day, of which Sir William Whiteway was Prime Minister and Sir Robert Bond the Colonial Secretary and the member for the Trinity district, was first notified late Saturday night about the events that were unfolding in Trinity Bay. The telegraph offices of outport Newfoundland were closed at the time, as they usually were on Saturdays and Sundays, and the first information the Government received was from a Captain Noble who, upon receipt of a message received at the St. John's railway station, went to the home of the

Colonial Secretary and relayed the news. The Government took its first action the next day (Sunday) when they dispatched the steamer, the *D. P. Ingraham*, to the scene.

A furor ensued in St. John's shortly afterward in which the opposition parties and a large cross-section of the general public accused the Government of being insensitive and callous to the plight of the people of Trinity Bight with its slowness in taking action. The Government insisted it had acted with all due haste, and countered with charges of political opportunism and mud-slinging.

In retrospect, it is difficult to support the accusation that the Government did not react as expeditiously as it should have to what would turn out to be a disaster of enormous magnitude. The intelligence that they had received on Saturday evening, they argued, was sketchy at best and provided no real indication of the true scale of the tragedy. It wasn't until they received more extensive and more accurate information on Sunday morning that they became fully apprised of what had happened the day before. Even then, the rescue effort was delayed for a short while by negotiations with the owners of the steamer, the *D. P. Ingraham*, which was dispatched to Trinity Bay only to find that she couldn't penetrate the ice-field which by then stretched across the entire mouth of the bay. Quick arrangements were then made to have the more powerful steamer, the *Labrador*, with a medical officer on board, sent to the area. But the *Labrador*, like the *D. P. Ingraham*, could not make an entrance into the bay because of the ice blockade, and after almost thirty hours of trying to force a passage through the ice, was obliged to give up and return to St. John's.

Regrettably, therefore, those great vessels with their

powerful engines and maneuverability, were unable to assist in any significant way in the search and rescue effort. The only large vessel of any kind that had been able to make a meaningful contribution was the schooner, the *Rosscleer*, which had already been inside the ice-field at the time of the disaster. The Government and the general public were loud in their praise of the good work that Captain Richard Fowlow and his volunteer crew had done in searching the bay for two full days immediately following the disaster.

The supposed slow reaction of the Government was, in effect, a moot point. Even if they had sent a steamer on Saturday evening, the Government claimed, it wouldn't have made any difference because the ice conditions by then would have prevented entry into the bay and the vessels would have been unable to undertake their mission in any case. Still, this explanation failed to satisfy the opposition and the general public, and the cries of shame and outrage continued.

Sir Robert Bond, the member for the Trinity district and who would later go on to become the Prime Minister of Newfoundland, paid a personal visit to the scene of the disaster. He had known many of the victims personally, and had been so devastated by the massive loss of life in his district and overcome with emotion when first announcing the terrible news to the House of Assembly, that he couldn't continue and a fellow politician had to break the news to the House in his stead.

Still, the arguments, charges, and counter charges continued on without abatement for days and weeks on end. They would only finally cease in July of that year when the Government's full attention, and that of Newfoundland in general, was suddenly preoccupied with another disaster – the Great Fire of 1892, the horrific conflagration that leveled much of St. John's and left more than twelve thousand of its residents homeless.

A hundred and ten years later, Trinity Bay is a vastly different place than it was at the time of the disaster. The population of the bay has more than quadrupled since the disaster and the area is now connected to the rest of the world by sophisticated telecommunication and transportation systems of all kinds. Ribbons of paved highway now join all the settlements to each other and to the rest of Newfoundland, and with a drive of only an hour or two, residents of Trinity Bay can board a flight in Gander to take them anywhere in the world. The town of Clarenville, which at the time of the disaster was a fledgling settlement of a handful of families and had played no role at all in what had transpired, is now the bay's largest and fastest growing community.

Some of the settlements of Trinity Bight, in particular the town of Trinity, have become great tourist attractions, renowned for their historical significance and hospitality. During the tourist season, busloads of people from all over Canada and the United States flock there every day for the scenery, to whale-watch, to take advantage of the myriad outdoor recreational facilities, and to take in the Trinity Pageant and other popular plays and dinner theaters. The area has also been the location for the filming of a number of Hollywood movies, including *The Shipping News* and *Random Passage.*

Many of the earlier place names have been changed; Ship Cove and Robinhood are now the town of Port Rexton; Champneys East, Champneys West and Champneys Arm together are now what was once called Salmon Cove; Cuckhold's Cove has been renamed Dunfield, and Trinity South, as a separate entity, no longer exists and has been incorporated into the town of Trinity. Some of the fishing settlements that existed in 1892 have disappeared altogether. The residents of Ireland's Eye were all relocated to other parts of Newfoundland by the Liberal Government's Resettlement Program of the 1960's and 1970's, along with a number of other nearby settlements such as Kerley's Harbour, Pope's Harbour, and British Harbour – and there is little evidence of any kind to indicate that the tiny fishing settlement of Green Bay, on the north shore, ever existed.

Today, despite the recent moratorium on codfish, the fishing industry – now focused on other species – is still the mainstay of the Trinity Bay economy. These days, however, it is done from the relative safety of large trawlers and forty to sixty-foot long-liners that routinely travel two hundred miles or more out into the open Atlantic in all kinds of weather, sometimes staying at sea for weeks at a time. Even the inshore fishermen, in their modern fibre-glass skiffs equipped with powerful inboard or outboard motors, sonar, floatation devices, and survival gear, can brave rough waters in comparative safety to tend to their traps and trawls. Very few fishermen today, though, continue to participate in the Province's dwindling seal fishery, which has been decimated by the world-wide efforts of protest groups and animal rights associations. Still, when the ice makes its annual appearance in the bay, many of the locals are unable to resist the temptation to take a "quick dart out to try to get a bit of seal meat and a feed of flippers."

With the passage of time, the words on the few headstones of the victims of the February 27th, 1892 disaster that are still standing have mostly been obliterated by the weather or have faded into illegibility, and the names and the stories of the twenty-four men who perished in the bay have long since faded from memory. Still, while the history of Newfoundland is replete with many large-scale fishing and sealing disasters at sea, the Trinity Bay disaster ranks among the largest such occurrence in which so many landsmen died at one time.

Appendix I

The following newspaper accounts of the Trinity Bay disaster have been reprinted and retyped as they appeared in the *Evening Telegram*, February 29th, 1892 edition.

Appendix I

Latest by Telegraph.

Awful Disaster

IN TRINITY BAY

By Saturday's Storm

TWO HUNDRED MEN

While Out Sealing Are

Driven Across the Bay.

Terrible Suffering.

MANY FATAL RESULTS

Over Thirty Missing

(Special to the *"Evening Telegram."*)

Seventeen Land.

Heart's Content, 11:30 A.M., To-Day.

Yesterday about noon seventeen men landed from the ice at Heart's Delight. They would have drifted even farther but that a woman observed them and parties immediately started out to their aid; others were reported visible at some distance off, but apparently frozen or exhausted. The rescued men reported that there were about two hundred men in the neighborhood of Trinity on Saturday when

The Storm Burst Upon Them,

jamming the ice and raising so heavy a sea that they found it impossible to make for the shore in their boats, and they were compelled to take refuge on the ice, on which they drifted till yesterday. These men had five boats with them, and burnt two to keep themselves warm, or they would have frozen to death Saturday night, which was intensely cold, the thermometer being

Down To Zero, and Blowing Hard.

What these men must have suffered is fearful to contemplate. From Heart's Delight another boat was visible, her crew being apparently frozen or exhausted. Relief parties immediately brought these in, and it is hoped that all on this shore will be saved. Some must be badly frozen, as Dr. Anderson was sent for at eleven o'clock last night, and has not yet returned. The startling intelligence was wired to St. John's last evening, and the Hon. Colonial Secretary was

Immediately on Hand.

Your correspondent received a telegram asking full particulars; the state of the ice in the bay, and whether it was possible to send steamers to the rescue this morning. The names of the rescued men were wired to Trinity, and a reply, just received, states that thirty or forty are missing, and that ten were frozen to death, some having died after reaching the shore. I have just heard from Old Perlican that five men landed there all right.

FROM OLD PERLICAN.

Five Men Land at Daniel's Cove.

(Special to the "*Evening Telegram.*")

Old Perlican, 11:30 A.M.,

Seventy men left English Harbour in boats on Saturday morning, for the purpose of hunting seals. Martin Bugden, William Penny, senr., William Penny, junr., Edward Bugden and Francis Barnes landed at Daniel's Cove, well, on Saturday evening. The others have not been heard from.

NEWS CONFIRMED.

Additional Particulars.

BODIES of 12 MEN

Brought in by a Schooner. First News From Rev. T. Atkinson Yesterday.

Messages to the Hon. Colonial Secretary confirm the disastrous tidings conveyed in our Heart's Content message of the casting away of the sealing crews from the north side of Trinity Bay. The first intimation came to him at ten o'clock last night from Captain Noble, who informed him that he had received a message through the railway officer, stating that the Rev. Thomas Atkinson had returned from Heart's Delight to Heart's Content, and had reported a list of five boat's crews of seventeen persons landed there (Heart's Delight), who had been driven out of English Harbour; they were badly frost-bitten; and that they reported two hundred men as being out in the bay all night, having been

Driven Off the North Side of the Bay;

and that another boat was seen off Heart's Delight. Immediately on hearing this, the Colonial Secretary despatched a message to the Government Superintendent of Telegraphs to get communications open with all points from Trinity to Heart's Content at once, and he telegraphed Mr. Austin at Heart's Content that two hundred men had been reported as having been driven off on the ice from the north side of the bay, and to telegraph full particulars after he had seen the Rev. Mr. Atkinson, informing him (Hon. Colonial Secretary) of the state of the ice in the bay, and whether it was possible for a steamer to proceed there. An hour and a half later he received a message from the Rev. Mr. Atkinson, giving full particulars, and stating that seventeen men had been

Landed at Tickle Harbour Point;

that they had made use of the seals for food while adrift, and had broken up their punts to make a fire. A message had also been received at eleven o'clock last night by the Colonial Secretary from Dr. Anderson of Heart's Content, stating that he had been called to see twenty-four Trinity men who had just landed at Heart's Delight. This morning the Colonial Secretary received a message from Mr. Austin of Heart's Content in reply to his of last evening, confirming Doctor Anderson's message that twenty-four men had been landed at Heart's Delight; that no other boats' crews were visible from the point; that the bay was clear of ice from Heart's Delight to Heart's Content, but was blocked from the latter point out.

A Schooner was Observed from Heart's Content under sail out in the bay, probably searching for the missing men. A message received by the Colonial Secretary from the magistrate states that the dead bodies of twelve men were landed there from a schooner. The Hon. Colonial Secretary at once entered into negotiations with the owners of the steamer *D.P. Ingraham* for the despatch of that steamer to the rescue of the castaway men, but, owing to the ice, he was informed that that steamer could not undertake the work; whereupon he promptly endeavored to have the sealing steamer *Labrador* go upon the service, and by this time that ship is no doubt on her errand of mercy; and if she is not it is not his fault. The fact that the outport telegraph offices were shut out of communication Saturday night prevented the intelligence being sent here immediately following the fatal event, and the despatch of assistance yesterday.

A PUBLIC MEETING

In Aid of Bereaved Families

We would suggest that a public meeting be held as soon as possible for the purpose of raising a fund in aid of the families bereft of their bread-winners. A similar course was adopted a few years ago in the case of the sufferers by forest fires at Little Bay, and with the most satisfactory result. The present call for aid is much more urgent, and we are confident our kind-hearted citizens will liberally respond in this case also.

Appendix II

The following newspaper accounts of the Trinity Bay disaster have been reprinted and retyped as they appeared in the *Evening Telegram*, March 1st, 1892 edition.

Appendix II

LEGISLATIVE PROCEEDINGS

HOUSE OF ASSEMBLY

The Trinity Disaster.

Speech of the Hon. Colonial Secretary

Monday, Feb. 29th, 1892.
The House opened at 4 o'clock.

The Hon. Colonial Secretary – Before proceeding to the order of business, it was his sad duty to intimate to the House that the Government were in receipt of information from the district of Trinity Bay of the occurrence of one of the saddest calamities that have befallen that community for a very long period. It is to the effect that some twelve men have been brought into Trinity harbour, dead; that twenty-four have reached Heart's Delight in a deplorable condition from exposure and suffering; and that seventeen others were found at Tickle Harbour Point, in a similar condition. It is supposed that altogether two hundred persons were exposed to the inclemency of the weather on Saturday and Sunday nights, and it is with the greatest fear and the deepest anxiety that the Government look to the result of future tidings respecting the fate of those still missing. He could hardly give adequate expression to his feelings of mingled sorrow and alarm. Representing, as he did, the people of the afflicted district, and knowing many, if not all, of the unfortunate men he was stunned by the great and sudden blow that had fallen, and was deprived of the power of expressing the sentiments he really felt. Nothing had been left undone by the Government to ascertain the fullest details of the disaster. He, Hon. Colonial Secretary, telegraphed to all the stations in Trinity Bay – he did so immediately on hearing the first intelligence of the terrible event – and took immediate steps to engage the services of a steamer, and send assistance to rescue the missing crews. He succeeded, after some little delay which was unavoidable in negotiating with the owners of steamers, in despatching the steamer Labrador to the scene of the disaster with a medical officer on board. The captain had been commissioned to search the district and bay for those still missing, and any further information received will be placed in the hands of honorable gentlemen, if applied for, and be communicated to the local press. He was directed by His Excellency the Governor to convey to the House His Excellency's condolences on this calamitous event, and his sympathy with the stricken people. His Excellency has also intimated that, if it was deemed desirable to open a subscription list for the benefit of the relatives of the deceased, he would be pleased to head the list with a substantial amount. He (C. S.) was sure that the House would cordially appreciate the warm sympathy and spontaneous generosity of His Excellency, and he felt certain that all hon. gentlemen would heartily respond to any appeal that might be made on behalf of the relatives of those who had been so suddenly taken from their midst. He warmly joined in the proposal that a subscription list be opened for the benefit of the sufferers. These men belonged to the class to whom we all owed, so much, and upon whose efforts the country is so largely dependent, that he would ask the House to manifest its sympathy with the people of Trinity Bay, in the heavy anguish of the present hour, by adjourning over until Thursday next.

Remarks of Mr. Morison.

Mr. Morison – In rising to second the motion he felt that he could add nothing to the force of the observations which had been so touchingly made by the hon. Colonial Secretary. The calamity came so suddenly and was so widespread; the interests affected were so important and vital that he felt at a loss to express his full sense of sympathy with those affected by the disaster. He was glad to give the Government credit for having taken up the matter so promptly, and for their desire to afford all possible relief to the unfortunate sufferers. Calamities at the seal-fishery there have been before, but none so melancholy as the present one. Men have been drowned at the ice; losses of vessels and sealers have occurred; but in this particular instance we have just been told that a large number of our fellow-creatures had been cast adrift upon the ice, some of whom had died from exposure to the weather, others had been landed in a deplorable condition, whilst no tidings had yet been heard of the remainder. This was a calamity unprecedented in the history of the country. Such a heart-rending story filled them all with the deepest sympathy, and he felt the House was actuated by a sincere desire to afford the afflicted survivors all the assistance and relief that lay in its power. He would therefore, as an expression of sympathy, second the motion for the adjournment of the House til Thursday next.

The House adjourned until Thursday next, the 3rd of March, at 4 o'clock.

Latest by Telegraph

Trinity Disaster

FOWLOW's SCHOONER

Arrives in Port With

TWO DEAD BODIES.

16 Men from Heart's Delight

REPORTS FIRES AT CHAPEL HEAD.

Four Men Still at Shoal Bay.

Telegrams to Sir Wm. Whiteway.

In response to telegrams, yesterday, from Sir William Whiteway, to Mr. Cole, Magistrate at Trinity, the following messages have been received:–

Trinity, Feb. 29, 1892.

Hon. Sir W. V. Whiteway:

"Yours received at 4:30 p.m. William Ivany and four sons, Herbert John Barnes, Charles, Jacob, Isaac, Nathaniel and Reuben Penny, Josiah and William Ivany, William and Albert Batson, Arthur Fifield, Patrick Hanlon and three sons are at Heart's Delight under treatment of Dr. Anderson. The missing are Isaac John Beston, William and Arthur Beston, Reuben Pottle, George Nurse, Henry, William, Charles and Solomon Penny, John Moores and two sons. The dead are James Penny, Tobias Penny, of Robert, Martin Beston, William Barnes, of Bernard, John Penny, Edward Pottle, Thos. Butler, of Thomas, William Stockley, Charles Day, Robert Bannister, Charles Bannister.

"G. H. Cole"

Trinity, March 1, 1892.

Hon. Sir W. V. Whiteway:

Fowlow's schooner has returned. She brings two dead men, found on ice, and sixteen from Heart's Delight.

"G. H. Cole"

(Special to the "*Evening Telegram.*")

Condition of Survivors.

Heart's Content, This Afternoon.

The actual number of men landed on this side is twenty-seven; that is, seventeen at Heart's Delight, four at Shoal Harbour, five at Daniel's Cove, near Old Perlican. The latter five are at Hant's Harbour to-day, whence they will endeavour to reach home in skiff when the ice moves. The others are still at Heart's Delight and Shoal Harbour, and all doing well. The one with frozen feet was saved from the necessity of amputation by prompt and

Sensible Treatment With Snow-Water.

The Colonial Secretary telegraphed last night to let everything possible be done for survivors. Hant's Harbour reports seeing a schooner near there last evening, but no further discoveries or arrivals are yet reported. Trinity Bay is blocked with ice from its mouth to Hant's Harbour and from Heart's Delight to the head of the Bay. Rantem reports being blocked, with edge of ice sixteen miles distant; no sign of missing men. It is feared that they were driven off on the outside of ice, and the only hope is that the steamer may find them.

LABRADOR SIGHTED

To Mr. Webber, M.H.A.:

Trinity, 11:30 a.m., To-Day,

Fowlow arrived at 9:30,

bringing sixteen of the men from Heart's Delight, all well. The crew of the schooner picked up the bodies of John Nurse and Solomon Penny in a boat off Scilly Cove. Captain Fowlow reports seeing fires on Chapel Hill, near Norton's Cove, but ice prevented landing. Four men are still at Shoal Bay, above Heart's Delight. They were unable to join Fowlow. Others from Old Perlican are gone to Hant's Harbour. The steamer *Labrador* has just been sighted.

Latest by Telegraph.

500 DOLLARS

For the Trinity Sufferers.

Munificent Generosity.

Shortly before going to press the Hon. Sir W. V. Whiteway received the following telegram from Austin R. Whiteway, Esq., M. A., Barrister, London, a relative of Sir William:–
London, This Afternoon,

Self and friends send $500 for late disaster. Authorize raising fund here.

"WHITEWAY."

MORE TRINITY NEWS

Names of Missing Men

A TELEGRAM received by Mr. Webber, one of the members for Trinity District, contains the names of the missing men there. They are as follows: Isaac Batson, Wm. Batson, Arthur Batson, Reuben Pottle, John Nurse, Solomon Penny, Geo. Nurse, Charles Nurse, Henry Nurse, William Nurse, of English Harbour and Salmon Cove. John Moores, Jacob Moores and George Moores of Trinity, South Side.

Message to Mr. McGowen.

In answer to a message of inquiry from John McGowen, Esq., of this city, Collector Doyle of Trinity telegraphs to this effect: "The Hunts are safe. There are thirteen persons still missing, including three of the Moores from here."

Telegram from Mr. Batson

Mr. Henry G. Batson, of Trinity, who was out in one of the boats when the storm broke upon them, telegraphed to his father here: – "We reached the Horse Chops. Martin Batson died after landing."

FROM SAFETY TO DANGER.

An Incident of the Trinity Calamity.

A Passenger's Fate.

A GREENSPOND man, who had been sick in the hospital most of the winter, took a passage for home on the S. S. *Labrador*. She being unable to arrive at her destination by reason of the heavy ice encountered, turned her prow from it. On Saturday morning she ran close alongside

One of the Trinity Bay Sealing Boats,

between four and five miles off Salmon Cove. The skipper's name was Nurse. The passenger elected to be put on board of Nurse's boat, in preference to again coming to St. John's, intending to work his way thence to Greenspond. One of the boat's crew asked Capt. Hann for a berth and was given one. The captain steamed away,

Not Thinking of Danger.

He, however, kept the boat in sight as long as possible, and saw no signal whatever. Although the captain thinks the boat got ashore, fears are entertained for her safety. Only by the light of the subsequent events can it be seen how wise it would have been to take that crew on board the steamer.

Appendix III

The following newspaper accounts of the Trinity Bay disaster have been reprinted and retyped as they appeared in the *Evening Telegram*, March 2nd, 1892 edition.

Appendix III

QUEEN SYMPATHIZES

With Trinity Bay Sufferers

TELEGRAMS TO HON. R. BOND

From the Secretary of State

THE LATTER SENDS £10.

Note from Hon. Colonial Secretary

Colonial Secretary's Office,
St. John's,
Newfoundland,
March 2nd, 1892.

Sir,– I have the honour to forward to you herewith copies of two telegrams just received from the Right Honorable Secretary of State for the Colonies, to which you will please give publicity.

I have the honour to be, sir,

Your obedient servant,
R. BOND, C.S.
Editor *Evening Telegram.*

Telegram Received from Secretary of State, 1st March.

(Copy).

Her Majesty commands me to inform you Her Majesty has heard with much regret intelligence of disaster to fishing fleet and to express her sympathy with injured sailors and relations of those who have lost their lives. Be good enough to send full particulars for Queen's information.

Telegram Received from Secretary of State, 1st March

(Copy)

I desire to express my deep sympathy with families of unfortunate fishermen who have lost their lives. Accept from me ten pounds for families. Will be paid to Union Bank of Newfoundland to relief fund.

S.S. "Labrador"

Returns.

BESET BY HEAVY ICE.

Stopped at Grates Cove

The North Easter Springs Up.

The steamer *Labrador*, Captain Hann, arrived at 11:30 a.m. from her cruise in search of the missing crews of Trinity Bay, but, unfortunately, owing to the prevalence of the north-easter and the packing of the drift ice, the vessel could not get much beyond Grate's Cove Point, the southern terminal promontory of Trinity Bay. There was no possibility of getting the steamer up the bay, Captain Hann stating that the ice was of a very heavy description, and left

No Chance of Ranging

in the mouth of the bay or in the area where the punts drifted. This latter would be well up the bay; in the offing from Hant's Harbour to Heart's Delight. Yesterday at 5:00 p.m., Captain Hann, when near Grate's Cove, sent a man ashore to despatch a telegraph message here that the steamer was then at that point and that the ice-barrier forbade the hope of her getting much further on her cruise. This morning the same unfavorable conditions prevailing, the captain gave up the search and returned to port. On Monday when the steamer left, what little wind there was came from the south'ard and

To this Circumstance

is due the fact that Fowlow's schooner was able to sail over the Bay, and effect the good work done. Yesterday the wind came up from the north again, and jammed the ice; today the strong north-easter makes the floe impenetrable. From the "crow's nest" the look-out swept a circuit of observation thirty miles in extent, but no trace of the unfortunate men , nor of their boats, could be discerned. The cause of the fires on Chapel Head has no doubt been discovered by the settlers in that neighborhood, and the telegraph office will keep us informed of future tidings, tidings we trust that will swell the numbers of those who have been happily delivered from peril.

THE COMMUNITY SHOCKED

By the Opposition Organ's

VICIOUS UTTERANCES

Over the Trinity Disaster.

A Piece of Political Rascality.

Editor "*Evening Telegram.*"

Sir,–the feelings of the whole community were shocked and outraged beyond expression by the publication of the remarks, in last evening's

Herald, relating to the Trinity disaster of Saturday last. It is really too bad that anybody should be so vitiated as to attempt to turn such an unusually heartrending calamity to political advantage. Such a

Hot-Headed, Heartless Misanthrope

as the Herald writer deserves to be banished from the region of journalism without further delay. It is enough for the narrow-souled and stunted mind of the Herald man to know that Hon. Mr. Bond is the Methodist representative of Trinity district. The Herald editor's creed is that "no good can come out of Nazareth." He will antagonize everybody, and

Gloat Over Misery and Distress

without the least regard for broken hearts and human feelings crushed to the last degree by one of the greatest calamities that ever happened in this country. In his mad infatuation to wring the hearts of the sufferers and intensify their sorrows, he says: "The news of the disaster reached the Government at 7 o'clock on Sunday, and that a steamer might have been started at 10 o'clock on Saturday night on the search for the missing men." The correspondent, "Sympathy," in the same issue of the Herald – probably the writer of the editorial – is simply

Infamous and Blasphemous.

The frantic election appeals of this vile sheet in the midst of its hypocritical expressions of sympathy, are almost enough to make one's hair stand on end. No wonder that

The Whole Community is Crying "Shame

on the Evening Herald," to endeavour to make more poignant the sorrows which are even now unbearable. There is only one redeeming feature in connection with the affair, and that is that the managers of the Herald give no countenance whatever to the remarks alluding to the Trinity Bay disaster. Yours, in deep sympathy,

PUBLIC OPINION
St. John's,
March 2, 1892.

TOUCHING REFERENCE

Of the Rev. Mr. Morton

TO THE TRINITY DISASTER.

Sorrow and Gloom

Editor "*Evening Telegram*."

Dear Sir,– during the service in the basement of George St. Methodist Church, last evening, the Rev. Mr. Morton made a touching reference to the disaster which has just occurred in Trinity Bay and which has brought sorrow and gloom to the hearts and homes of so many persons in that neighborhood. He could imagine the

Anguish and Distress

experienced by those who where the sufferers in the heartrending calamity – the Rachels weeping for their loved and lost, and "refusing to be comforted because they were not." It brought to his mind an event which had happened within a mission in which he had formerly been employed – an explosion in a mine by which seventy persons came to their end. It was

A Dark Day for the Place

in which that sad event happened. The gloom and distress which overspread that locality and filled so many homes would not very soon be forgotten. He felt deeply and acutely on behalf of the sufferers in Trinity Bay. His warmest sympathy went out for them, and his earnest prayer was that the great "disposer of events" would afford that divine consolation to the bereft families which alone could assuage their trouble and help them through the trying ordeal in which, by an inscrutable want of Providence, they were now placed.

Yours truly,

St. John's, March 2, 1892.

R. P.

Appendix III

Latest by Telegraph.

Trinity Disaster.

Running for Their Lives

ACROSS TRINITY BAY

Through Slack Ice

THEY ARRIVE AT FOUR P.M.

When the Storm Came.

(Special to the "*Evening Telegram.*")

Heart's Content, To-day.

The five men who landed at Daniel's Cove were in slack ice when the storm came on about 11 a.m. They rowed towards their homes for about an hour and a half, when they got to clear water, and found their boats could not live. They bore back for the south side of the bay, and had slack ice to row through till they got a quarter of a mile from Daniel's Cove, when they hauled their boat over the ice and arrived there at 4 p.m. on Saturday. Their clothing was wet and frozen, and they say that, in that condition, they could not have lived on the ice till ten o'clock that night. Three of them were in a boat of ten feet keel; the other two in a boat of eight-and a half feet keel. They saw the punts that put into Heart's Delight,

Put Up Sails and Steer,

about west. Also, before the storm came on, they saw four or five boats out to the eastward of them, chasing seals til they got out of sight, and they think that, if those crews were not swamped, they must have driven south of the ice and perished. They also spoke to one Henry George Ivany half an hour before the storm sprung up; a nephew of one of them was in the punt with Henry George Ivany. The names of the five (who manned the two punts mentioned and landed at Daniel's Cove) are: Martin Bugden, Edwin Bugden, Francis Barnes, William Penny, and James Penny. A Scilly Cove man out hunting yesterday

Saw a Drifting Punt

and in it a powder-horn, gaff, and two oars. He also reported seeing a steamer down near Heart Point, making back and forth, in about a space of three miles, til nightfall, when she steamed eastward. The men landed at Heart's Delight have gone home. The mouth of the bay is still jammed with ice.

From Dr. Anderson.

Heart's Content,
Feb. 29, 1892.
Dear Mr. Bond,–

There was nothing to necessitate the expense of telegraphing you, so I didn't wire this morning as intended. At Shoal Harbour I found William Ivany of English Harbour, and his three sons; the father had his fingers and toes slightly "seared;" James had both feet and the lower parts of his legs completely frozen, but they had been judiciously attended to, and the ultimate loss may not be greater than the tips of his heels, the balls of his great toes, and the ends of some of the toes; his fingers had been severely nipped. Mark was

Supposed Dying When Brought Ashore.

He had to be carried in a sail; I found him in bed with reaction established, and all the toes of both feet black and blistered. He seems likely to lose the skin of them at least. Walter had fingers, toes and one ear damaged. At Heart's Delight were sixteen men, most of them scathless, several with fingers blistered. The Shoal Harbour men were wet, and had no fire; the others managed to light one and keep it going. They used the fragments of a boat and some seal pelts. All are quartered on people who this time of the year are "short" but the

Visitation is Cheerfully Borne.

I fixed up the injured parts of the Ivany family and others in the manner best to second what had been done. The dressings will suit for some days, at the end of which the real extent of the damages will be determinable. Some spoke of setting out to walk home. I should say all those from Heart's Delight might do so if provisioned, but they would suffer. I do not see how James Ivany and Walter possibly could, and should be very doubtful about their father and brother.

Yours, & c.
(Sgd.) W. ANDERSON

Appendix IV

The following newspaper accounts of the Trinity Bay disaster have been reprinted and retyped as they appeared in the *Weekly Record*, March 5th, 1892 edition.

Appendix IV

Weekly Record

SATURDAY, MARCH 5, 1892.

HAVOC ON THE SEA.

Terrible Loss of Life.

Desperate Struggles.

HAIR-BREADTH ESCAPES.

Heartrending Scenes. - Heroic Acts of Rescue. - Thirteen Men Dead. - Eleven Still Missing.

The air is full of farewells to
the dying,
And mournings for the dead;
The heart of Rachel for her
children crying,
Will not be comforted!

The week that has passed since we last placed our little journal into the hands of its many readers has brought to this town and the neighboring settlements a terrible calamity; and it is our painful duty to-day to record what had proved the direst catastrophe ever known in the history of Trinity, - surpassing as it does in point of individual and general suffering, hair-breadth escapes, heartrending tales and scenes, anything of the kind ever heard of by the oldest inhabitant. Many terrible accidents have occurred, fraught with great loss of life; but none have been attended with such terrible circumstances as that of Saturday last. As we begin this short sketch of the terrible affair, we realize to the fullest, our utter inability to give anything like a satisfactory report. Many of our readers are already aware of the bare facts of the disaster; but few besides the residents of the immediate neighborhood, and the eye-witnesses of some of the scenes, can recall it in all its awful details.

For two or three days previous to Saturday the 27th ult. there had been quite a number of seals shot in the Bay. Saturday morning dawning fair and everything looking favourable for a successful day's seal-hunting, the majority of the seal-hunters from Green Bay on the one side to Ireland's Eye on the other side were up betimes and away in their boats in search of seals. So anxious were some of them to be away early that they took very little food before leaving and many were but thinly clad. The sea was smooth, air warm, little or no wind, and several seals were shot by some of the further off boats. All went well until about 11 o'clock, when the wind accompanied by intense cold, suddenly changed, blowing with terrible force from the N.N.E. With the rising gale the sea was soon lashed into foam. The majority of the boats were some miles off the land when the squall struck them, and they saw that to reach where they had left in the morning was an impossibility, entailing as it would a desperate row in the teeth of the gale. Some of the crews, however, belonging to Robinhood, Salmon Cove and English Harbour, who were not far off the Horse Chops (which lay nearly dead to windward) determined to make an attempt to land on that part of the shore. Six crews began the desperate task; and after five hours desperate rowing, the spray continually drenching them, freezing as it fell and covering them with ice, they reached the shore. The majority of them were so exhausted and benumbed they had not strength to get out of their boats. In two cases the poor human frame was unable to bear up under the terrible strain on nerve and muscle, and before land was reached they succumbed. One crew broke their oars and were drifting helplessly to leeward, when, with utter disregard for their own safety, and at the risk of sinking their boats with the extra burden, another crew took them on board. It was on board this boat that the first poor fellow died. So heavily laden was the boat with the eight men, and the ice that was constantly forming on her sides, that to prevent her from swamping and drowning all, the body of the dead man was committed to the sea. Shortly after, the second poor fellow, (a brother of the first victim) succumbed from cold and exhaustion. The scene after land was reached baffles description. Four other men succumbed here from exhaustion and intense cold shortly after landing. From

Appendix IV

John Butler, of Robinhood, who was an eye-witness of the proceedings, a Record representative obtained the following account of the tragic events at Horse Chops; the narrator, with the modesty which is characteristic of the true hero, passing lightly over the grand and noble acts of self-sacrifice and valor he himself performed. Had it not been for his incessant attention many of the poor fellows who landed at the Horse Chops, and who were in the last stages of exhaustion and paralyzed with the intense cold, would undoubtedly never have recovered. Here is what he said:–

"I went to English Harbour on Saturday last to attend the funeral of my wife's brother, Joseph Penny, who had died a few days before. When the storm came on I did not go to the funeral, but went out on the Horse Chops to see if any of the boats were coming. Half way out to where the boats landed I met Robert Penny and Robert Ivany, of English Harbour who had also been out looking for returning boats, but seeing none they were going home. I got them to go back with me. We waited for half an hour, saw no sign, and then made a fire a little distance back where some brushwood was growing. Stayed by the fire about half an hour, and then I went out to the edge of the cliff over Hay Cove again. I saw Henry G. Batson's boat coming slowly towards the land, the men in her hardly able to make a stroke. Looking down over the cliff I saw several other boats had landed in the cove, and I saw my brother Alexander trying to get William Stockley up the hill. I ran down and took my nephew James Butler on my back and after a time got him to the fire up on the hill. The two men belonging to English Harbour were working also to get some of the men up the steep gulch. All of the men who landed here were covered with ice, hardly able to move. Two had died before landing, and four died after they landed, two of them near the fire and the other two down the hill. Robert Bannister managed to get partly up the hill and I saw him, while I was trying to bring some of the others to life, on his hands and knees unable to move. He just muttered, God bless us, and died. His son died just before. We did all we could to help the men who landed there, but there were not enough of us to help them all, and we saw some die quite near us while we were unable to aid them. Only three of us were there to help all who landed. It was a terrible time. Stephen Day of Robinhood came about half hour before dark, and did a great deal to help the other men, even taking off some of his clothes to put them on some of the other men. He and I carried my nephew to Wm. Ivany's at English Head (the nearest house) about 2 miles away. He was unconscious all the time but after a long time we managed to get life in him and he recovered. His left foot and right hand are frost bitten. My brother Alexander has both hands frostbitten. He gave his mitts to the boy. Out of the crews who landed at Horse Chops six men died."

This is just an outline of this man's story. Want of space prevents us from publishing it in full. Some of the details are heartrending in the extreme.

While these scenes were being enacted at Horse Chops, others of a like nature were taking place further up the shore. The crews who decided not to attempt to keep too far to windward landed at Trouty, Bonaventure, Ireland's Eye, Thoroughfare, and some at Deer Harbour. All of them were terribly exhausted and coated with ice. Many had to be assisted from their boats at each place. Those who landed at Trouty and Bonaventure recovered without any loss of life. Many were frostbitten and much exhausted, and but for the incessant attention of the residents of the places would undoubtedly have died. Among those who landed at Ireland's Eye one man, Wm. Barnes of English Harbour had died in his boat before landing. Another of the same crew was unconscious and had to be taken from the boat. All the others were well cared for at the house of Mr. Thomas Cooper and ultimately recovered. The Ireland's Eye men (to their credit be it said) who had only escaped a few minutes before with their own lives, hearing that many boats were out from Salmon Cove and English Harbour, organized a volunteer search party and in spite of the heavy gale of wind and the intense cold went out to the adjacent islands in search of supposed missing men. One of the rescuing party gives us the following account of what they did and saw: Learning that a large number of English Harbour and Salmon Cove boats had been caught in the storm and knowing it was impossible for them to land near their own homes, a volunteer crew was called for and readily obtained to search the islands near for any who might have landed there. Two boats were manned and started. One returned without any sign of men or boats. As the second was returning about 6 p.m. a fire was seen in Thoroughfare, about a mile from Ireland's Eye, and they immediately went to see what it meant. The sight that met their eyes baffles description. Around the fire were five men, two nearly dead, the others trying by all means in their power to restore them. A boat was by the shore and in her were the bodies of two young men who had died before land was reached. The rescuing party took the rescued and carried them to the nearest house (Old Tilt) where they were well looked after. The bodies of the dead men were put in coffins to be taken home. It was a task that unnerved the strongest man.

Early on Sunday morning a crew of four men went to Rider's Harbor and other near places to see if any had landed there. No one was found. About this time a search party arrived from Trouty and Ship Cove looking for missing men. Just as they were leaving Ireland's Eye a boat was met with five men on board coming from Deer Harbor. Three boats had reached there on Saturday, and two men of the number had died before landing.

The story of suffering and death told by the survivors who reached there, was the saddest of all the sad tales, and the poor fellows who told it wept like children. On Monday the bodies of the men who were landed at

Thoroughfare and Ireland's Eye were brought to Trouty and from thence conveyed to their homes.

Although the events recorded above happened on Saturday, no one in town was aware that such a terrible loss of life had occurred until Sunday afternoon. Great anxiety had been felt all Saturday night for some of the men who were out but, as so many had landed in safety, it was hoped the others had escaped with a "drubbing," and had reached harbor further up the shore. Early on Sunday, however, intelligence was received of some of the events noted alone, and throughout the day other stories were brought from different places near, each, as it became known, increasing the magnitude and horror of the disaster. By Sunday evening it was known that out of the two hundred (about) who were caught in the storm, eleven deaths had occurred, and nearly forty were still missing. A private telegraphic message received for English Harbor late on Saturday night became known on Sunday afternoon. It told of the safe arrival at Old Perlican of one of the missing crews. That little missive was hailed as a message of hope for others of the missing.

When the Telegraph Office was opened on Monday morning, numerous anxious enquirers thronged the doors, countless messages were dispatched to, and received from, all parts of the country. The news of the disaster spread like wildfire. Early in the day a message from Heart's Content stated that about twenty men and boys had landed at Heart's Delight and vicinity. Words fail to describe the cheering effect of that message. Despairing faces again looked cheerful, and other heartbroken sufferers whose dear ones were still missing were filled with hope for their safety.

The number missing on Monday night was thirteen men and boys, and nothing more was heard until Tuesday morning when the schooner *Rosscleer*, Captain Richard Fowlow, which had been searching the Bay since Sunday, returned to port. Her report was soon known.

Sixteen of the men who landed on the South Shore of the Bay were on board, also the bodies of John Nurse and Solomon Penny which were picked up on Sunday in their boat off Scilly Cove. Both bodies were under the thwarts of the boat, and it is thought the poor fellows rowed until exhausted and then laid down to die. The number of missing was now reduced to eleven, – the death roll contained thirteen names.

From Patrick Huilan, one of the men who landed at Heart's Delight, we learned the following account of their hair-breadth escape:

"I was out on Saturday with my three sons. When the squall struck as we were about half way between Horse Chops and Hart Point on the South Shore. We put up our sail and made her lie as close to the wind as we could, so as to get a distance in the Bay in case the wind should come further off-shore. The spray was continually going over us and freezing and we soon saw it was impossible to reach land on the North Side of the Bay without running the risk of freezing to death. After a time we gave her a little sheet and ran her for a pan of ice. Got out on the pan, and made a fire to get something to eat and drink. Just as we were doing this a sea broke over the pan and washed everything off except ourselves, and filling one of the smallest boy's boots. We had to jump in our boat and run her before the gale until about 4 in the afternoon when we sighted some more boats in the ice. Just before dusk we reached the other boats. There were four boats, and twelve men when we got there. We all hauled up our boats on a large pan, turned up the larger boats to make a shelter from the wind, and made a fire. I had two seals in my boat and we pelted them to burn the fat, breaking up one of the smaller boats also to use as fuel. We were on the ice drifting up the Bay all night. It was bitterly cold in spite of the big fire, and we were dancing and jumping all night to keep up our spirits and to keep from freezing. At dawning we were about five miles from land off Heart's Delight. We hauled our boats over some ice and then rowed for land which we reached about 9 o'clock. The people treated us with wonderful kindness, doing all in their power to relieve us. None of us were badly frozen. William Ivany of English Harbour and his three sons landed a little farther up the Bay about 4 in the evening. They had been on the ice all night and had to be hauled ashore in a dory. They were rescued by men from Heart's Delight at risk of their lives. One of them was badly frozen but all were doing well when we left. They could not get down to where Captain Fowlow took us in and it was impossible for the schooner to get to land or remain longer where she was, as the ice was making fast. We all wish to thank the good people of Heart's Delight for the kindly attention they gave us. Under Providence they saved our lives, and we shall never forget their kindness to us – strangers in a strange place."

Captain Fowlow's gallant deed was feelingly mentioned too, by this man and he desired the thanks of the rescued to be publicly conveyed to Captain Fowlow. Indeed, the thanks of the whole community, nay, the thanks of the whole country, are due to this noble man and his crew. At the risk of losing his schooner this brave man and his hardy crew scoured the Bay in search of missing men and we trust they will not be forgotten.

The Ireland's Eye and Heart's Delight men, too, deserve commendation. Their promptness it was in going to the assistance of their suffering fellow-creatures, that saved a number of lives. Less heroic acts have been awarded the V.C. But to particularize the many acts of valor performed during this dread disaster would be an impossibility. Brave acts of self-denial, gallant deeds of rescue at risk of life are heard from every quarter. They will have their reward!

Promptly after hearing of the disaster the Government dispatched the steamer *Ingraham* to search the Bay for missing men. Owing to the heavy ice in the Bay she was obliged to retreat. A more powerful steamer, the *Labrador*, with Dr. Pike on board, was then despatched, but after thirty hours were spent in an unsuccessful attempt to force a passage, she too was obliged to return to St. John's. Search parties from the shore at the head of the Bay have been sent out, but up to the time of writing, no news of the eleven missing ones have been received. Their sorrowing friends have been hoping against hope that some of them will return. Alas! it seems a forlorn hope, and the general opinion now is that they have gone to "that bourne from which no traveler returns."

The names of the dead are: Solomon Penny, of Wm., John Nurse of Wm., belonging to Green Bay; Martin Batson, of Geo., Tobias Penny, of Robt., James Penny, of Robt., Edward Pottle, Wm. Barnes, of late Bernard, belonging to English Harbor; John Penny, of Chas., Charles Day, of Samuel, belonging to Salmon Cove, West; William Stockley, Isaac J. Butler, of Robinhood; Robert Bannister and Charles Bannister of Ship Cove.

Those still missing are: Isaac John Batson, Wm. Batson, of Richard, Arthur Batson, of Richard, Reuben Pottle, of English Harbor. Charles Nurse, William Nurse, Henry Nurse, George Nurse, (sons of Wm. Nurse of Salmon Cove.) John Moore, George Moore, Jacob Moore, of Trinity South.

Upon such a small community as ours where all the dead and missing men were well known, this catastrophe has had a terribly crushing effect. Woe and lamentations are heard on every side. Heartbroken widows and orphans, fathers and mothers who have lost their promising sons, have suddenly appeared in our midst. In several cases every male member of the family has been taken. A depressing funereal stillness has come over us. The funerals of the deceased have been largely attended; the solemn burial services of the different churches being listened to with more than ordinary interest and awe. Strong men of iron nerve, unable to bear up, wept like children. But all is not awe and sorrow. Many are able to realize that those taken from them by the cruel relentless sea, are "not lost, but gone before" to that

Haven–"where tempests cease And surges swell no more."

Now that the first bitter pangs of the loss are over the burden of life must be taken up again. And this is a harder matter that many realize. Some of the deceased have left behind them helpless widows and children, aged fathers and mothers for whom some provision will need to be made. And in this we are glad to say that many kindly sympathizers at home and abroad have given substantial evidence of the sincerity of their sympathy. A subscription list has been opened in St. John's, headed by His Excellency the Governor, and it is hoped that a sufficient fund will be realized to provide the needy with the means of beginning life anew, – for that is what it means to many.

Throughout the whole of the country, a wonderful feeling of sympathy has been manifested for the sufferers. The House of Assembly adjourned from Monday until Thursday. His Excellency the Governor who was giving a dinner at Government House, postponed the event as a mark of sympathy. Messages of condolence and sympathy have been dashed from all over the world. On Wednesday, Her Most Gracious Majesty the Queen, who is ever in sympathy with all of her suffering subjects throughout her vast Empire, telegraphed, through Lord Knutsford, a message of condolence and asked for full particulars of the disaster. These tokens of sympathy coming at a time when the heart is crushed and broken, when even life seems hardly worth keeping, have been wonderfully cheering and gratefully received.

We, too, in concluding this hastily-prepared sketch, beg to tender the heartfelt sympathy of the RECORD to the bereaved; commending them, with all sincerity, to the care and guidance of the all-pitying Father. In no more suitable words can we conclude than by quoting the following beautiful stanzas from the poet Longfellow's *"Resignation:"*

Let us be patient! These
severe afflictions
Not from the ground arise.
But of ten times celestial
benedictions
Assume this dark disguise.

Appendix IV

There is no Death! What
seems so is transition;
This life of mortal breath
Is but a suburb of the life
Elysian,
Whose portals we call Death.

And though at times impetu-
ous with emotion
And anguish long suppressed,
The swelling heart heaves
moaning like tho ocean
That cannot be at rest,

We will be patient, and assuage
the feeling
We may not wholly stay;
By silence sanctifying, not
concealing,
The grief that must have way.

Appendix V

The following newspaper accounts of the Trinity Bay disaster have been reprinted and retyped as they appeared in the *Weekly Record*, March 12th, 1892 edition.

Appendix V

Further Details Anent Recent Disaster

Captain Fowlow's Report.

Dear Sir, – The following is a short account of our doings while out searching Trinity Bay on Sunday and Monday, the 28th and 29th ult.

On Sunday morning two men from English Harbor came to me to know if I would go out in the Bay in my schooner to have a look for missing men. The schooner was all ready, having been fitted out a day or two before to proceed to the seal-fishery as soon as a time offered. I immediately hoisted my flag and soon had a volunteer crew. By half-past ten we were under weigh. We sailed out to the Horse Chops, and from thence to the edge of the ice, – about two miles from the Chops. We ran along by the edge of the ice, which carried us nearly over to Old Perlican, without seeing anything worthy of note. A lookout was kept on the mainmast head with a spy-glass all the time. We then left the ice, and ran up the shore in the direction I thought anything would drift the night before, keeping 3 and 4 men in the rigging all the time. When we got up abreast Hant's Harbor, and about two miles from the land, we came across a punt's peggin, an oar and a spread belonging to some swamped punt. We saw nothing more until we ran as far as Scilly Cove. About a mile from there we saw a punt full of water, rounded the schooner to, and sailed up near the punt. In her we found two dead men, Solomon Penny and John Nurse. We took the bodies on board and laid them out in the hold. This was about 3 o'clock in the afternoon. We ran on again, with every eye on board on the look out, as far as Heart's Content. We thought to get in there, but could not for ice. Seeing we could not get in anywhere on the South Side of the Bay, we shaped our course for Upper Deer Harbor. I intended to search the ice further up the Bay next day, but on our way across we saw a smoke rising at Heart's Delight, which we knew was a signal for us. Hove around and reached in for that place, but ice prevented us from getting in to land. Night coming on, we reached across the Bay again for Deer Harbor, which we reached at 11 o'clock in the night. We were at work again next morning at dawn; but the ice had frozen fully an inch thick while we were anchored and we were obliged to break it with punts on each side of the schooner. After a time of hard work we got clear, and sailed across the Bay as far to windward as the wind would allow, spying in every direction all the time. On the way across the Bay I spied from the main-mast head two boats on the ice a long distance to windward. Being unable to reach them in the schooner, I sent a crew away in a punt to get to them and bring back whatever men they could find, dead or alive. By 2 o'clock, p.m. the wind became very light, and seeing I could not get to the land in the schooner, I sent away another punt and 4 men to row to land, trying all the time to work the schooner nearer to land and in the direction I had sent the first punt. The first crew returned about half-past three, and reported the boats on the ice deserted. We concluded from that that the men had reached the land, and that was the cause of the signals made to us on Sunday. After our crew got aboard we ran to leeward around a point of ice, and got as near the land as the ice would permit, when we spied our second punt and three others coming from the land. I knew at once they were some of the men we were in search for. When they came alongside I was delighted to find there were 16 men alive and well. They had been rescued by the Heart's Delight people the day before. Being then late in the afternoon, the drift ice running down the shore, we made all speed to get clear, to avoid being "nipped" on the straight shore. By dark we were clear of the land. I intended to beat farther up the Bay, but finding it impossible to do so owing to ice, I shaped my course for Trinity, which we reached at 9 o'clock on Tuesday morning, after a hard night's work breaking ice to get the schooner through.

Thanking you for the space, I am,

Yours truly,
RICHARD FOWLOW
Master schr. *Rosscleer*
Trinity, March 5th

Appendix V

Statement of William Day.

Saturday February 27th I left my house about seven o'clock with my cousin, Charles Day, to go out in the Bay in search of seals. We rowed off in the Bay until we was about 3 and a half miles off the Horse Chops when observing dark clouds rising to the Northward we turned our boat and rowed for the Horse Chops that being the nearest land. There were several other boats near us, John Moore, John Bannister and John Wells and another two-handed boat, George Ivany of English Harbor, alongside of us. All the punts rowed for the Horse Chops but the four-oared punts rowed away from us, with the exception of George Ivany who kept near us. We rowed for about two hours, and our punt becoming frozen up with the water continually coming over her, and being in an exhausted condition, we saw that there was no hope of getting in to the Horse Chops. George Ivany then put up his sail and headed her in the Bay. He was about one hundred yards to the windward of us then, so we signaled to him and he took down his sail and came down to us. I said "we have no sail, so let us all go together in one punt." Considering my punt to be better than his he took his sail and paddles and got in with us. There were four of us now in a little punt about ten feet keel and the nearest land we had any hope of getting to was fully sixteen miles from us. We put up our sail and headed her in the Bay not knowing what moment would be the last. We almost filled her two or three times but managed to free her again. The water was all the time coming over us, which, with the intense cold, was piercing. Our little boat got frozen up and she wouldn't make any way ahead, so I took a powder horn and pounded the ice off as well as I could. George Ivany steered her with a paddle crouched down in the stern of her, while Charles Day rowed one paddle when not heaving water, which occupied most of his time. The other man, Edward Pottle, had to lie down in the bottom of her amidship, and the water and slob would be up around his legs sometimes. I stood up and looked out for pans of ice as long as I could stand, and then had to kneel down in the water on the sheets and look out. We were all near exhausted with cold and wet and scarcely able to speak when George Ivany said "I see the land," which cheered us up very much. This was Bonaventure Head, about two miles to windward of us. Shortly after I missed Charles Day's paddle, he was rowing behind me, and looking around I saw his hand going as when he was rowing. I knew at once that the poor fellow was dying, and the next moment he fell backwards on poor Pottle, who was still lying in the bottom of her. I took him hold and begged him to try and live a few minutes longer as we would soon be to land, but he did not answer me and never spoke again. Poor Pottle lost his cap, so we put a jacket over his head and he would keep asking us if we were near land. We cheered him up as well as we could but he was frozen down in the bottom of her, with the other man dead across him, as we did not have room to move him in one small punt. He was continually getting weaker, but we were very near the land when he died. We got to the entrance of Irelands Eye Harbor, but had not strength to row in so we kept away for the Thoroughfare. We saw another punt coming in to leeward of us and we both reached the land together. We asked him where he belonged. It was John Hiscock of Salmon Cove, although belonging to the same place we were frozen up so much and frostbitten we did not know each other. We had two men dead in our punt, and he had two men given up in his. We were not able to row in the Thoroughfare, and had to land out on the point about a mile from the nearest house, John Ivany's, Old Tilt. When we landed we were almost all alike, one scarcely able to help the other. Fortunately John Hiscock had some dry matches and got a fire, while I started for John Ivany's to try and get some help for the others. I had to go over hills and rocks and through woods, sometimes I would get exhausted altogether and wouldn't be able to see. Then I would stop for a few minutes and get revived again. God only knows how at length I reached John Ivany's, just at dusk. I said to him "go to the Thoroughfare Point as quick as possible, you will find men there some dead and some alive." He went on at once and soon returned with the living men. By that time there was a boat got there from Ireland's Eye and brought in the dead bodies. Our warmest thanks are due to John Ivany and sons, as I believe them to be the means under God of saving our lives on dreadful day.

The people of Ireland's Eye acted nobly towards us doing all in their power to help us, even fitting out a punt to bring us home, but slob prevented them, so they landed us in Trouty. We got home about sunset on the following Monday. I pray God never to let me pass through the like again.

WILLIAM DAY.

Sources

Encyclopedia of Newfoundland and Labrador
Smallwood Heritage Foundation,
Harry Cuff Publications Limited, St. John's, Nfld., 1994,
Volume Five.

The Evening Telegram, St. John's, Newfoundland,
February 29th, March 1st, and March 2nd, 1892 editions.

Goin' To the Ice, Michael Harrington,
Harry Cuff Publications Limited, St. John's, Nfld., 1986.

Department of Tourism, Culture and Recreation
Provincial Archives Division–Colonial Building,
Military Road,
St. John's, Newfoundland.

The *Weekly Record*, Trinity, Trinity Bay, Newfoundland,
March 5th and March 12th, 1892 editions.

Photo Credits

The Provincial Archives of Newfoundland and Labrador

PANL A 12-58: A sailing and rowing fishing punt (page 101)

PANL B 4-150: Schooner in growlers (cover and page 102)

PANL A 8-132: Sealers working on loose ice (page 102)

In the mid to late 1700's, a group of desperate men, mostly deserters and escaped prisoners, as well as indentured men and boys who had run away from their fishing masters, secluded themselves in the wilderness on the Southern Shore of Newfoundland's Avalon Peninsula. Led by Peter Kerrivan, himself a deserter from the British Navy, these renegades, predominantly Irish, established their hideout on or near the Butterpot, a small mountain about nine miles inland from Ferryland. Defying the law and evading all attempts made to capture them, they survived on the great caribou herds that roamed the barrens and by raiding the fishing settlements along the coast. Known as the Society of Masterless Men, their legend is one of the most exciting and daring in Newfoundland's rich and colourful past.

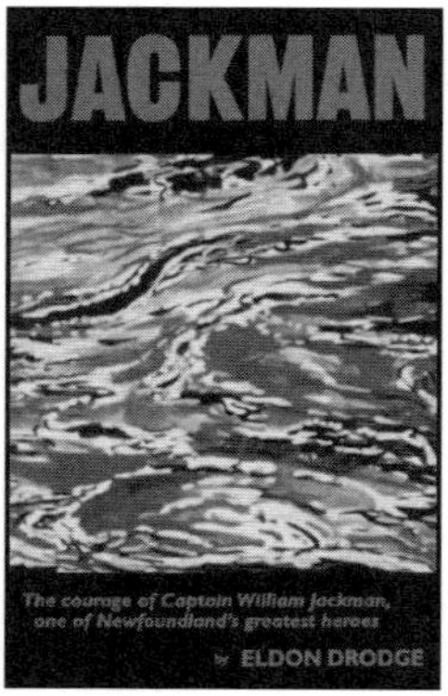

At the height of the devastating October gale of 1867, a small schooner, the Sea Clipper, was driven onto a reef at Spotted Island, Labrador. Already seriously damaged from an earlier collision with another schooner, she was being pounded to pieces by the raging sea. The twenty-seven people on board faced certain doom. Miraculously, a young sea-captain from Renews, William Jackman, appeared on the scene to undertake one of the most amazing sea rescues ever known, and to earn for himself the Silver Medal of the Royal Humane Society of London and the undying adulation of the people of Newfoundland and Labrador.

ELDON DRODGE was born in Little Heart's Ease, Newfoundland, but has spent most of his life in St. John's. He retired in 1997 after a thirty-five year career in the computer industry. He now resides with his wife, Joan, in Torbay where gardening, painting, and woodworking are among his many hobbies. A long-standing sports enthusiast, he still plays old-timers hockey and spends countless hours at the hockey rinks and soccer fields watching his grandsons play.

His many boyhood holidays spent "around the bay" with his grandparents and aunts and uncles filled him with a great love for outport Newfoundland and its glorious past. His first book, *Jackman,* and his second, *Kerrivan,* both retained a great following. *Peril on the Sea,* is Drodge's third novel continuing his exploration of Newfoudland's rich cultural history.